IN THE
TYCOON'S DEBT

BY
EMILY McKAY

MILLS & BOON

First published in Great Britain 2009
Paperback edition 2010
Harlequin Mills & Boon Limited,
Eton House, 18-24 Paradise Road, Richmond, Surrey TW9 1SR

© Emily McKaskle 2009

ISBN: 978 0 263 87762 5

Set in Times Roman 10½ on 12¾ pt
01-0110-43593

Harlequin Mills & Boon policy is to use papers that are natural, renewable and recyclable products and made from wood grown in sustainable forests. The logging and manufacturing process conform to the legal environmental regulations of the country of origin.

Printed and bound in Spain
by Litografia Rosés, S.A., Barcelona

IN THE
TYCOON'S DEBT

For my darling Henry,
the boy who'll put anything in his mouth,
from old Cheerios, to shiny new pennies,
and even the occasional computer key.
Thanks for spitting out my K.

Prologue

Fourteen years ago

They were less than five miles from the county line when Evie Montgomery saw the flashing red-and-blue lights in the rearview mirror. Beside her, Quinn McCain cursed, something he rarely did in her presence.

Evie leaned across the console of her BMW M3 to glance at the speedometer and then at Quinn—her husband of exactly three hours and forty-seven minutes.

They'd had it all planned out for weeks now. The morning of her seventeenth birthday, they'd sneak out early, drive to the courthouse and get married in a simple ceremony. Once they were married, nothing would keep them apart. Not her father's archaic ideas about social class. Not his father's drunken negligence.

"You're not speeding," she said. "Why are they pulling you over?"

The skin around Quinn's mouth had tightened, pressing his lips into a flat line. He gripped the steering wheel with both hands, his knuckles white. Quinn was driving, even though it was Evie's car—the one her father had bought her for her sixteenth birthday. As if the cost of the car could make up for the fact that the present was three weeks late, since he never remembered the actual date of her birth.

Quinn, of course, didn't have a car. His father had a rusted-out Chevy up on cinder blocks in front of the aging RV where they lived. A month ago, Quinn had scraped together enough money to buy four used tires from Mann's Auto, where he worked after school. He'd spent weeks trying to get the Chevy to run, only to give up when he couldn't afford a new alternator. He'd cursed then, too. He'd so wanted to drive his own car when they went to the courthouse.

That stubborn pride of his was one of the things she loved most. That and the fact that, in a town of almost twenty thousand people, he was the only person who saw her as more than just Cyrus Montgomery's daughter, who imagined she might want more than a life of hermetically sealed wealth and perfection.

Dread clutched her stomach. "Why are they pulling us over?" she asked again, more because she hoped he'd come up with a reasonable answer than because she believed he would.

Quinn slowed the car from a very respectable fifty-four in a sixty zone down to fifty, and then forty-five. "Maybe you have a taillight out?"

"I don't." With every twitch of the speedometer needle, her pulse ratcheted up a notch. "Don't pull over," she ordered impulsively.

The car had slowed to just over thirty. "I have to pull over." Quinn sent her a piercing look. "Evie, what's going on?"

She struggled to put into words the indistinct fear gnawing at her. "If you pull over, something awful will happen."

"What?" he pressed.

"I don't know. But something bad. I just know it. This has been too easy. I'm sure my father will do something horrible, like have you arrested or something."

"I haven't done anything wrong," he argued logically. "Sheriff Moroney wouldn't arrest me."

"My father practically owns this town. He'll have his cronies do whatever the hell he wants them to do."

"That's not—"

"Legal? No, it's not. It's reality." And she'd learned not to underestimate her father's sheer determination. "He'll pull us over. Find some excuse to search the car. Maybe say it's been stolen. Something. They'll plant evidence. Maybe it'll even stick."

"This is what you've been worried about. Why you encouraged me to get the Chevy working."

She wished she could deny it, but panic clawed through her. *What if I'm right? What if they find a way to keep us apart? What if I've come this close to happiness and it's going to be snatched away?*

"I can't just keep driving," he pointed out, obviously trying to be the voice of reason. "I'll have to stop sometime."

"You don't have to stop in Mason County." Her voice was thick with resistance. With a lifetime of pushing against her father. "We've got a full tank of gas. You can drive into Ridgemore, and pull into the parking lot of the police station there."

But even as she said the words, the glare of the flashing lights behind them became brighter. Evie looked over her shoulder in time to see a second squad car pulling onto the road behind the first.

Ridgemore was at least twenty minutes away. If Quinn didn't pull over before then, they'd assume he was running from the police. She'd seen car chases on TV. Seen drivers pulled from cars and beaten.

"I'm pulling over now," he said quietly. "Sheriff Moroney is a reasonable man. I've known him my whole life. I'll talk to him. Besides, we have to face people sometime. It might as well be now."

"No, we don't. We can just leave. After we stop in Ridgemore, we can go anywhere. Dallas. L.A. London. Anywhere."

"We can't go anywhere." It was the one point of contention between them. "You haven't even graduated high school and we have two hundred dollars between us. Besides, I can't leave my father." Quinn gave her a hard look. "I can take care of you."

"I know that." They were married now. Nothing would ever come between them.

"It'll be okay. We'll be together soon."

He said the exact same thing every time they were together, just as they were saying goodbye.

"We'll travel somewhere far away where we don't even speak the language," she said, as she always did. It was all part of the elaborate fantasy they'd spun. "We'll drink coffee in a little café by the park and order foods we can't pronounce."

"We'll stay in the best hotels," he added.

"We'll drink expensive champagne."

"And I'll shower you with diamonds," Quinn said quietly as he flipped on the turn signal and pulled onto the shoulder.

"And I'll shower you with love," she said sadly. All the while, her heart thudded painfully in her chest. She prayed she was just being paranoid.

Before Quinn could even open the door, she jumped out of the car. "Sheriff," she began, but he cut her off before she could voice her protest.

"Stay out of this, Evie."

"No."

Sheriff Moroney leveled a stern look at her. His mouth was pressed into a disapproving line. "This doesn't have anything to do with you."

"What is this about, sir?" Quinn asked, stepping from the car.

"You're going to have to come with me, Quinn."

"Why?" she demanded. "He hasn't done anything."

The sheriff didn't meet her gaze but stared at Quinn, a silent warning in his eyes. "That car you're driving's been reported stolen."

Shock tore through her. "This is my car," she insisted. "It wasn't stolen."

"It's your father's name on the title, Evie. Don't make this harder than it has to be."

"You can't do this. I won't let you." She reached out a hand toward the sheriff, not realizing one of the deputies had snuck up behind her.

She didn't know if he was merely overzealous or had just misinterpreted her actions. When she reached for the sheriff, the deputy snagged her around the waist, pinning her arms to the side and lifting her clear off the ground. She yelped in protest.

Quinn launched himself toward them, but the sheriff was too fast. He clipped Quinn with a knee to the stomach and an elbow to the shoulder. Quinn went down hard. Her anguish made her mad with rage. She bucked against her captor, kicking, screaming. All to no avail. She couldn't break free. She couldn't help Quinn.

She watched, helpless, as the boy she loved, her husband of less than four hours, was yanked from the ground, shoved into the back of the sheriff's car and hauled off to jail. She pleaded with the sheriff, the deputy, anyone who would listen.

No, she hadn't been kidnapped. No, her car hadn't been stolen. No, she'd never before seen the gun they claimed had been in Quinn's pocket. No, she didn't know how he could have gotten his hands on her mother's diamond necklace, which they also claimed to have found on him.

They didn't let her see him. They didn't let her call a lawyer for him. They didn't so much as hand her a tissue.

She waited for hours in the front room of the jailhouse. Then, just before midnight, her father walked in. Calm, peaceful and completely in control. And willing to make it all go away. Quinn would walk free. On one condition. All Evie had to do was sign the annulment papers her father had had drawn up. Otherwise Quinn was looking at five to ten years in a federal prison.

So she signed the papers.

It was a hell of way to spend her seventeenth birthday.

One

Quinton McCain was known by his business competitors and his employees for being extremely intelligent, devilishly handsome and unnervingly even-tempered. In fact, he so rarely displayed emotion that quite a few rumors—and the occasional bet—had circulated around the office regarding his past, about which no one knew anything.

Since he had little interest in office gossip and even less in people's opinion of him, he did nothing to encourage the rumors—but nothing to put them to rest, either. One rumor painted him as a trained assassin for the CIA. Another as a Black Operative for a secret branch of the military. A third as the billionaire heir to a national chain of automotive stores. None of the rumors mentioned a wife. For most people, it was easier to imagine Quinn as a ruthless killer than a loving husband.

Which was why, the day Genevieve Montgomery called his secretary asking for an appointment and claiming to be his ex-wife, the rumor mill went into overdrive. By the time Quinn found out about the appointment, there was nothing he could do to stifle the gossip.

By the time Wednesday morning rolled around, the situation was so desperate that before Quinn could even sip his coffee, Derek Messina let himself into Quinn's office. Messina Diamonds, McCain Security's biggest client, was located in the same building just a few floors up. So while it appeared Derek hadn't particularly gone out of his way to stop by, it didn't bode well that he'd taken time out of a workday to do so.

Quinn scowled, trying to send subliminal get-the-hell-outta-my-office signals. Subliminal only because saying it aloud would make him seem way too preoccupied with Evie's impending visit. "So I take it you heard."

"About Evie?"

Quinn nodded. "Based on how quiet it gets every time I enter a room, it's all anyone in this office is talking about. A good portion of my employees are former military. You'd think I wouldn't have to put up with this crap from them."

He wasn't the kind of guy who made many jokes, but usually when he did make them, his friends had the common courtesy to laugh. It seemed a very bad sign that Derek simply studied him.

"Your meeting with her is today, right?"

Since he couldn't get Derek to take a hint, Quinn leaned back in his chair and nursed his coffee. "In just a few minutes."

"Do you know what she wants?"

"Don't know. Don't care."

"Do you want me to stay?"

"When she's here?" Quinn asked in disbelief. Derek nodded, seriously. "No, but I'd really appreciate it if you could pass her a note in biology. Tell her to meet me out behind the gym after band practice."

Derek gave him a blank look, and it was a minute before Quinn remembered that Derek hadn't had a traditional upbringing and had never even gone to high school.

Quinn sighed. "I'm not fourteen. I don't need you to hold my hand when I meet her. You know how I feel about my marriage."

"Right," Derek said. "You don't want to talk about it. You don't want to think about it. If I wasn't such a good friend, you'd shoot me just so there'd be one less person in the world who even knew about it."

"I believe those were my words."

They were a little harsh—especially in light of all those "paid assassin for the CIA" rumors—but at the time he'd said them, he and Derek had been very hungover. Too much brandy the night before had been the culprit in both their confessional discussion and their hangovers the next morning. Since they were both wishing they were dead, the threat didn't seem like such a bad one.

"Is that her out in the waiting room?" Derek now asked.

"I don't know." He'd arrived at six this morning. Though he hated the notion that he'd been hiding inside his office ever since, he couldn't overlook that possibility.

The truth was, he didn't know how to feel about Evie popping up in his life after all these years. On one hand, it might be gratifying to have her see exactly how well he'd done for himself. On the other, every cell in his body recoiled at the thought of her. Of the reminder of what an idiot he'd been.

He'd loved her. Been completely, stupidly devoted to her, in the way only the young and naive could be. He would have done anything for her. And, bored rich girl that she was, she'd toyed with him, manipulated him and used him to get back at her father. All before breaking his heart, ending their marriage and leaving him to rot in jail.

"It might be good to see her," Derek pointed out. "It might be cathartic."

What could he say? That he'd rather crawl naked through a pit of scorpions? That he'd rather go through therapy on live TV? That he'd rather parachute into hostile territory? Hell, forget the parachute. He'd just jump out of the plane.

His expression must have spoken volumes because, finally, Derek said, "You know, you could cancel the meeting. You could refuse to see her."

"No. I can't. If I did that, everyone in this office would wonder why I canceled. Then there'd be more rumors and speculation. Or, worse, sympathy."

He could just imagine it now. Some "helpful" person would decide he'd canceled because it had been too hard on him to see his ex-wife. Then he'd have to put up with the cloying compassion. People being *nice* to him.

He was a CEO, for God's sake. He had a net worth that ranked him among the richest men in the state. Beside which—while not actually an assassin—he was an excellent marksman and trained in demolitions. Men who could blow stuff up should not be the objects of pity.

He stood, tugging at the hem of his suit jacket. "No, the only thing I can do now is just get this over with."

"What are you going to say to her?"

"Whatever the hell I need to say to get her out of my office and my life as quickly as possible."

Evie Montgomery had forgotten how much she truly despised wearing cashmere. It made the back of her neck itch.

But the twelve-year-old lavender sweater was the single most expensive item of clothing she had. So two days ago, she'd pulled it and the matching skirt out of the storage chest and aired it out, knowing that if she wanted to get through today with any semblance of dignity, she needed to look her absolute best.

Still, as she sat in the impeccably decorated high-rise

offices of McCain Security, she had to fight the urge to scrape her nails along the back of her neck. However, doing so would leave bright red marks across her skin. It was silly vanity, but when she saw Quinn for the first time in nearly fifteen years, she didn't want to look blotchy.

She was nervous enough as it was, without adding blotchy to her list of problems.

What if he never wanted to see her again? If that were the case, the next twenty or so minutes were going to be very uncomfortable. Particularly the part where she asked him to give her fifty thousand dollars.

Before she could contemplate that possibility, the door to his office opened and the same dour-looking man who'd entered ten minutes ago walked out. He gave her an appraising look, and she had the distinct impression he and Quinn had been discussing her. Which was just great. Because she wasn't nearly nervous enough as it was.

A moment later, the receptionist looked up and said, "Ms. Montgomery, Mr. McCain will see you now."

Evie moved mindlessly into his office, barely aware of his assistant asking if she wanted a cup of coffee and then leaving when she didn't reply. She was too keyed up to drink anything and too aware of Quinn to answer.

The instant she saw Quinn's face, Evie knew it had been a mistake to come. Knew her hopes that he'd moved on—maybe even forgiven her—were about to be crushed. His expression said it all.

He stood behind his desk, every muscle of his body tense, as if she were some medusa from his past who'd turned him into a statue of repressed hate. But of course, being Quinn, he didn't look angry that she'd come. No, he looked shut down. The way he used to look when dealing with "concerned" teachers who would try to talk to him about his father's drinking problem.

She was probably the only person in the world who knew that his complete detachment hid seething anger.

He had not moved on. He'd never forgiven her. And he would not loan her the money. Jeez, she'd be lucky if he didn't call in security guards to have her hauled out and thrown down to the curb.

A hysterical giggle bubbled up through her chest. Did the CEOs of security firms have security guards?

He certainly didn't look as if he needed them. In the years that had passed, his shoulders had broadened. His physique, which had always been long and lean, like a professional swimmer's, had bulked up.

No, he wouldn't need anyone else to throw her out. He looked more than capable of doing it himself. And like he might even enjoy it, if he let himself.

But she'd been doing hard things her entire life. This would be no different. Though undoubtedly more humiliating.

Since this wasn't going to get any easier, she launched into the script she'd been practicing for days. "Hello, Quinn. It's been a long time."

She expected some rejoinder. *Not long enough,* perhaps.

Instead, he nodded, his face still lined with cool distaste. As if a slug had slimed its way into his office and he didn't want to step on it and risk ruining the carpet.

"Evie." He accompanied the word with a brief nod.

That was the only way she knew it was a greeting and not a slur.

"How have you been?" she asked, mostly because it seemed rude to jump straight to the part where she begged him for money.

"Let's skip the pleasantries. You must want something from me or you wouldn't be here."

"You're right." She gestured toward the chair opposite Quinn's desk. "May I sit?"

He seemed to consider the question for a minute before nodding.

Maybe if they were both sitting, she'd be able to dismiss her fears that he was about to jump across the desk and pounce on her like a wild puma devouring his prey. However, instead of sitting when she did, he continued to lean, his hips propped against the edge of his desk, a mug of coffee steaming beside his hand. Since his legs were stretched out in front of him, she had to cross hers at the ankle and keep them tucked off to the side to avoid brushing her feet against his. If her mother were still alive, she'd be happy to know Evie was finally putting all of those deportment lessons to use.

"You must know that whatever it is you want, I won't give it to you."

"It's not for me, if that makes any difference at all."

"It doesn't."

The Quinn she'd known had spoken with a slight east Texas twang, not unlike the one that had made Matthew McConaughey the stuff of fantasies. Yet this Quinn had buried his drawl beneath the bland Midwestern tones of a newscaster. What else from his past did he keep hidden away?

Not that it mattered. She was here for one reason only. To save her baby brother. "It's for Corbin."

"I don't care—"

She spoke quickly over his arguments, her desperation palpable. "I need you, Quinn. You know I wouldn't ask for help if there was anyone else I could turn to." He didn't say anything, so she kept talking. "He's gotten himself into trouble and owes some people money. These people—the Mendoza brothers—I had a friend of mine who's on the force tell me about them. They—" She couldn't quite bring herself to repeat the things she'd heard.

Apparently the Mendoza brothers were the up-and-comers in the world of organized crime in Dallas. They were making a name for themselves by being more brutal and more ruthless than any of their competitors. They'd already been linked to a string of bloody murders, but the DA hadn't been able to build a case against them.

"Corbin says they've threatened him. They're going to cut off a finger or something. But I think he's wrong. I think it's going to be much worse. He's scared. And I'm scared for him."

So scared she couldn't let herself think about it. She'd been concentrating only on getting here. On talking to Quinn. On putting herself in his hands and hoping he'd help her.

Corbin was the only family she had left. Ever since

her mother had died when Evie was a teenager, her relationship with her father had grown more and more hostile. She couldn't lose Corbin, too.

For a brief moment, Quinn's gaze seemed to soften as he studied her. Then he straightened and rounded the desk, distancing himself from her. "So why come to me? I suppose you want me to take care of it." He made a sweeping motion with his hand. As if brushing Corbin's problems aside. "I suppose you think that because I own a security company I have a legion of hired thugs to do my bidding. But that's not the kind of work I do."

"I know what you do."

He quirked an eyebrow as if to say, *"Oh really? Prove it."*

"You make money," she stated succinctly. "Lots of it. I know what you're worth."

This time the other eyebrow went up, too. She'd surprised him.

"I don't want you to make his problem go away. I want you to pay off his debt."

"You need money." He spoke slowly, as if marveling at the irony. "And you have no one else to ask?"

Despite the embarrassment creeping under her skin, she forced herself not to look away. Not to shy away from his cool, appraising gaze. "There's no one else."

"Your father owned half the county."

She hadn't spoken to her father in more than ten years, but last week she'd gone to him and begged. Literally on her knees. She'd begged him for the money. And he'd said no. Spit it, actually.

Her father had made her childhood miserable with his obsessive controlling. He'd ripped happiness from her hands. He'd taken Quinn from her. If she could ask him for the money, then she could ask Quinn—who'd once loved her. Surely if she just explained…

"You know my father." She smiled gamely, hoping to stir up a little of the old camaraderie. "He doesn't approve of gambling. He disowned Corbin two years ago. Cut him off completely."

"And you can't loan him the money yourself?"

"He owes a lot." She sucked in a deep breath. Gut-check time. "Fifty thousand dollars. I could mortgage my house, but it'd be weeks before I saw the actual money, and frankly, it's not worth that much. I'd get maybe twenty or thirty thousand."

A slow, cynical smile toyed with his lips. "You want me to just hand you a check for fifty thousand dollars?"

"I know you have it."

His smile broadened without any humor reaching his eyes. "And why would I give it to you?"

"You have more money than you ever dreamed of. That's just a drop in the bucket for you."

"And why would I give it to you?" he repeated, more slowly this time.

She considered the question for a second, letting herself really ponder why she'd been so sure he could help. Willing him to meet her gaze, she answered as honestly as she could. "Because of our past, I suppose. Because once you loved me. Because once you swore you'd do anything for me. Because—"

"No." He straightened and rounded the desk.

As he lowered himself into his chair, she got the distinct impression she was being dismissed. Panic rose in her throat.

"That's it? 'No'?"

He looked up with a *you're still here?* expression on his face.

She'd worked so hard over the past decade to learn to control her rebellious impulses. In her line of work, a feisty temper did no one any good. But somehow, just being with Quinn stirred up all her adolescent defiance.

"Just, 'No'?" she repeated. She curbed her temptation to say more. She didn't know this new Quinn, but simple logic told her angering him wouldn't get her the money she needed. "I think you can offer me a little more than that."

"I'm a businessman, Evie. What exactly would I be getting in exchange for all this money I'd be giving you?"

She sucked in a breath of surprise. She hadn't expected this. Blind desperation had gotten her this far.

"I'll pay you back," she said stupidly, but he was already shaking his head.

"If you don't have the money now, how would you get the money to pay me back?"

"The mortgage," she threw out. "I'll start with that. And I'll make payments. I'll—"

But he shook his head. "No. I just don't think that's a good return on my investments."

He was toying with her now. Obviously he enjoyed having her at his mercy. It was a bit chilling really, that satisfied gleam in his eyes. This man before her was a stranger.

No, not a stranger. Nothing that benevolent. More like a thug on the street. One of the angry teenage boys who prowl around late at night, leering at people, looking dangerous and disreputable just for the sake of it. Hoping to scare just for the thrill.

Funny that Quinn had never been like that as a teenager. He'd been respectful. Shy, even. He was acting like this now merely to punish her.

She'd never been good at being bullied. It was why she and her father never got along. All of her frustration boiled up inside her, forcing its way out in a taut tone.

"If you want to be mad at me, fine, be mad. But don't take this out on Corbin. He's innocent in all this."

"If he has dealings with the Mendoza brothers, then he's far from innocent."

Everything in her stilled. "Then you know who they are?"

"I do."

"Then you know how desperate his situation is."

"I do."

"And you still won't help?"

"I don't see why I should."

He was back to the cool, clipped tone. She forced herself to look beneath it. To search for some chink in this wall he'd put up between them.

Somewhere beneath this cold facade of a man was the boy who'd once loved her. She just had to find the right words to unlock him.

She rounded the desk to stand before where he sat in his chair. Acting on instinct, she dropped to her knees before him, then cradled his jaw in her hands. His gaze was hard, but he wouldn't look her in the eyes.

His face had filled out since she'd seen him last. The planes of his face were just as angular, even though he'd lost the lean boniness of youth. Despite the hour, he already had growth on his jaw as if he'd risen early and hadn't bothered to shave before coming in. It prickled her palm. His skin was hot beneath her fingertips as if to foreshadow she was about to be burned.

Suddenly she remembered how they used to sneak into the shop classroom over lunch. How she'd sit on the counter, her legs wrapped around his hips. How desperate she'd be to kiss him, and he'd always just hold her first for a second. As if he was afraid she'd disappear if he didn't hold on tight enough.

Remembering that, she once again willed him to meet her gaze, and he did. For the first time since she'd entered his office, he seemed to really look at her. In that instant, all her fear for Corbin faded and she was lost in the pain of their past. Of all the things she'd never said to him. Before she could stop herself, it began pouring out.

"I'm so sorry, Quinn. I'm sorry for how things ended. For how I must have hurt you. You've got to know I never meant for any of that to happen and—"

He shoved the chair back and stood quickly, leaving her kneeling there before him. "And now you want something from me, so you're here to apologize."

She stood, bristling from the sting of his words.

"What exactly is it you want from me, Quinn? I've already apologized. Do you want me to beg?"

"You want to know what I want? I want retribution for what you and your family did to me. I want you—" he pointed his finger at her "—completely at my mercy."

"I *am* completely at your mercy." She planted her hands on her hips, meeting his gaze. "I have nowhere else to turn. No one else can help me."

He smiled, clearly pleased by the thought. Delighted at having her right where he wanted her. His expression left her with the unpleasant sensation that he'd been manipulating her into this very position.

"Fine," he said, crossing his arms over his chest. "Then I want the wedding night I never had. I want you in my bed for one night."

Numbness crept over her body as his words echoed through the room, her mind barely comprehending his meaning. "You want me to sleep with you for money? You want me to prostitute myself?"

"Think of it however you need to. But yes, that's what I want."

Part of him expected her to slap him. Or maybe to throw something at him.

Instead, she merely stared at him, looking as if she herself had been slapped. Her eyes were wide, her face pale with shock. But she didn't run. She didn't leave. Didn't do any of the things he expected her to do.

He had only made such an outrageous proposal

because he knew how she'd react. The Evie he'd known would never let a guy get away with saying something like that. She never backed down from a challenge. No one bullied her. When she got pushed, she pushed back. Hard.

So he'd propositioned her, knowing it would tick her off. Knowing it was the one surefire way to rile her temper and get her to storm out. But instead of angry, she looked confused. Hurt maybe. As if that was the last thing she'd have expected from him. And then—as if he wasn't already feeling like the asshole who was going around kicking puppies, damn it—he watched her expression as the full implication of his outrageous words sank in. Her cheeks pinkened delicately.

Yet still he didn't get the outrage he expected.

Every instinct in his body screamed at him to snatch back his words. The eighteen-year-old boy he'd once been reared his head, compelling the man he was now to protect her. He alone knew how much she hated being vulnerable. How much she hated asking for anything. He knew how hard this must be for her.

He wanted to go to her, wrap her in his embrace and rock her back and forth. To promise her he'd do everything in his power to keep her safe. To protect her. Forever.

And, damn it, wasn't that exactly how he got in this position in the first place? Hadn't this whole mess of crap started because he'd wanted to cherish and protect her? But when push came to shove, she'd rammed all his tender emotions down his throat. Evie didn't need any protecting. She was a user. And she was using him all over again. Luring him back into her knotted little web of lies and manipulation. And he was mere seconds from falling for it all over again.

What was he supposed to do? Ask her to leave? *Oh, pretty please, leave me alone so I can cry in private.* What was he—a thirteen-year-old girl?

He was better than this. Tougher than this.

He had to get her out of here. Now.

"That's my offer. Take it or leave it."

He held his breath. Praying she'd do what any sane woman would have done minutes ago: slap the arrogant grin off his face and storm out.

She didn't slap him. She merely pressed her lips into a disapproving I-expected-better-of-you-than-this line and turned and walked out.

He sank back in his chair as relief washed over him. She was gone. He'd never have to deal with her again. He could get back to his normal, sane life. Or so he thought.

Not fifteen minutes later, his office door swung open, banging emphatically against the wall from the force. Evie, looking grimly determined, marched back into his room and slapped a business card on his desk.

She glared at him as she bit out, "Here's my e-mail address. Let me know the time and place and I'll be there. Bring your checkbook."

A moment later, she was gone and he was left staring blankly at the cream-colored card.

Well, hell.

Two

By Friday evening at eight forty-two—approximately twenty-four hours after receiving an e-mail that read simply, "Your house, nine o'clock, Friday," Evie was beginning to wonder if she shouldn't rethink her strategy.

As she paced back and forth along the length of the living room, a single question haunted her: how the hell had she found herself in this situation? When she reached the center of the room, she took a detour around Harry, her aging arthritic greyhound. Evie reached the red velvet armchair facing the fireplace and sank onto the edge of its plush cushion, leaving plenty of room for the two cats, which were curled together behind her into a perfect yin and yang.

Annie, the black cat, mewled in protest. Oliver, the

gray cat, stretched out a paw and pushed at Evie's leg. She took the hint and stood, scowling at the useless creature. "You should be offering me comfort, not pushing me out of my chair."

Wasn't that just like a cat? You rescue them off of kitty death row at the animal shelter, you love them, shelter them, and in return all they do is complain that you're sitting on their chair. They were no help at all.

But the truth was, she'd gotten into this mess with Quinn in the same way she'd gotten saddled with three pets, all of whom had more ailments and illnesses than the average nursing home resident.

She was a sucker for the wounded.

It was why—over and over again—she'd stepped in to bail out her worthless brother. It was why she'd promised him she'd find a way to pay off his debt.

And it was why she'd agreed to meet with Quinn tonight.

Clearly, she and Quinn both needed closure. She wasn't fool enough to imagine that this bargain they'd struck was about anything other than revenge. Her family had hurt him. Punished him for loving her. She'd inadvertently made things worse on Wednesday. By bringing up how much resentment he must still harbor, she'd wounded his pride.

She knew all about wounded pride. All about the lengths people would go to save face. In her job as a social worker, she was constantly soothing people's egos. Manipulating them into accepting the help they needed. Struggling to see past the bravado to the person beneath. Which put her in the unique position of seeing straight through Quinn's awful behavior. Even though it was aimed at her.

She knew he didn't actually want her. This wasn't about sex for him. Which was all well and good because she certainly had no intention of actually sleeping with him. He just needed to play this farce out so he'd feel like he'd regained his dignity.

Apparently, the way their relationship ended had hurt him badly. But instead of getting on with his life— as she had—he'd bandaged over his wounds with the trappings of wealth and success. The injuries were hidden from most people, but they'd never healed.

If all went as planned tonight, she'd force him to confront the past. It would do them both good. They'd talk about their brief marriage like reasonable adults— after all, she was a certified mediator. She knew what she was doing.

He might resist as first, but eventually he'd see the benefit of hashing it all out. And maybe, just maybe, she'd be able to talk him into loaning her the money. Not giving it to her, and certainly not in exchange for…well, for anything. But a nice simple loan that she'd be able to pay off in…oh, about eighty or ninety years.

Her plan would work. It had to work. Because the alternative was unthinkable.

Not wanting to consider what that alternative might actually entail, she headed for the kitchen, looking for something to calm her jangling nerves.

At the back of her pantry, she found a half-empty

bottle of tequila left over from margaritas she'd served at her Oscar party. The doorbell rang just as she twisted off the cap. The sound froze her like a statue. Evie took a gulp straight from the bottle, grimacing as the tequila scorched its way down her throat and into her belly. She still felt its heat in her mouth a moment later when she opened the door.

He said nothing. Just stood there, the light spilling from her house not quite reaching his face, so his expression remained cast in shadows. That seemed appropriate somehow, since she was having so much trouble reading him.

"Hello, Quinn." Her voice sounded remarkably calm.

See how easy this was going to be. Just two adults having a reasonable conversation.

He looked her up and down, his gaze cold as he took in her jeans and button-up sweater. His eyes seemed to linger on her mouth, making her all too aware she'd been nervously gnawing on her lips all evening. An expression she couldn't read crossed his face. If she didn't know better—that is, if she didn't know how much unresolved anger he felt for her—she might have interpreted that look as desire.

She stepped back, allowing him room to enter her house. Instead of walking past her, he stopped mere inches away.

Her pulse inched up in response to his nearness. She wanted to believe it was nerves. Anything else was unthinkable. She would not let herself be attracted to this man.

Determined not to notice how good he looked, she asked, "Is there a problem?"

"Interesting neighborhood."

He said it like a slur. She lived in the eclectic south Dallas neighborhood of Oak Cliff. Her street was full of funky, aging houses, some of which—like hers— were being carefully renovated, and others of which hovered in a state of negligent disrepair. This part of town had a bad reputation, although it was far safer now than it had been a couple of decades ago.

"Thanks." She smiled, pretending to mistake his comment for a compliment, as she stepped aside and gestured for him to enter.

She was acutely aware that she—in her jeans and cotton sweater—looked right at home in the cozy shabbiness of her living room with its scuffed hardwood floors and yard sale antiques. But he—in his tailored business suit—looked strikingly out of place. Like a flyer from *GQ* got missorted into an issue of *Thrifty Nickel*.

"It's not exactly the kind of place I'd have expected Cyrus Montgomery's daughter to live."

"I like it here. And don't worry, your Lexus will be fine parked out on the street. Probably."

She shouldn't be trying to pick a fight with him, but she felt overly protective of her little bungalow, given that she'd done most of the renovations herself. And Quinn, of all people, should be able to look past an address.

He ignored her comment. He surprised her by reaching out a hand and plucking the hem of her sweater. The heat of his knuckle grazed the bare skin of her belly as he toyed with the fabric.

"For fifty thousand dollars, I would have appreciated a little more effort. Something silky maybe."

"On my salary, I can't afford any silky lingerie."

He quirked an eyebrow, a flicker of surprise registering on his face.

Immediately she cursed herself. That had *not* been the right answer. *Well, you big fat jerk, I've got a closet full of sexy underwear and you'll never see it.* Or maybe, *If you want to see the silky stuff, offer more money.*

Something—*anything*—that didn't make it sound as if she'd invited him here of her own volition. Like if she had a closet full of sexy peignoirs she would have worn one for him. As if the problem here was the inadequacies of her wardrobe or salary, not his behavior.

She opened her mouth to deliver a withering insult, but before she could pry one out of her subconscious, he nodded toward the bottle of tequila in her hand and asked, "Aren't you going to offer me a drink?"

Only then did she remember the tequila bottle. "I forgot I was holding it."

And then she wished she hadn't said that aloud, either. Dear lord, had she been cursed by some kind of verbal affliction? Worse still, when she spoke, he leaned toward her, obviously catching a whiff of alcohol on her breath. A wicked smile spread across his face.

"You were drinking before I got here. I must make you really nervous."

"That's what you wanted, isn't it?" she asked.

"You think I want to make you nervous?" he asked.

"Of course you do." Pleased that he'd been so easily deflected from talking about lingerie, she headed back toward the kitchen, not bothering to look and see if he was following her. "That's what this is all about, isn't it? That's what you said the other day. You want me completely at your mercy. You want me vulnerable."

She pulled two tumblers from the cabinet by the sink, all too aware of the sound of his footsteps behind her. She splashed tequila into both of the glasses and then held one out to him as she turned around.

He studied her for a minute before accepting the glass. "That is what I said."

Propping her hip against the kitchen counter, she searched his face for signs that he regretted his hastily extended bargain, taking in the lines of strain around his mouth, the tension in his muscles. She found none of the regret she'd been looking for.

Her kitchen was a galley stretching the back length of the house, with the fridge at one end and an old diner table at the other. Quinn seemed to dominate the narrow room. He stood between her and the door to the dining room, trapping her.

This new Quinn was tough and strong. Hard. His defenses mortared into place like the great crenellated walls of a castle. But he was leery, too. Restrained. Maybe wounded.

That was okay. She could see through his defenses. She'd just have to look hard.

"Let's cut to the chase," she said.

He quirked an eyebrow. "You want to skip the drink and go straight to bed?"

Okay. Look really hard.

"This isn't about sex," she said. As she spoke, she pushed past him, out of the kitchen and back to the living room, where the space was a little less cramped. Where she had more room to escape.

She'd only made it a few steps into the living room when he grabbed her arm and spun her around to face him.

"It isn't?" he asked.

"No." It was difficult not to feel disconcerted. After all, she was certainly used to talking about all kinds of intensely personal topics with strangers. But they were never topics that were personal to *her*. It was her job to be empathetic but dispassionate. Uninvolved. So she drank a swig of tequila before pressing on. "This is about revenge. My family screwed you over and now you want your pound of flesh."

Evie's words tore through the restraint he was trying desperately to hold in place.

She stood before him, bold as brass, no longer the polite, simpering miss she'd been in his office but the confident woman she'd been hiding underneath her demure cardigan twin set. Still, he could see only hints of the girl she'd once been. Her auburn curls fell about her shoulders in a tumble of waves, all reckless defiance. But she seemed to be tempering that blazing arrogance with mature moderation. He almost got the sense that she was trying to keep him at a professional distance.

Still her words rankled. "Your *family* screwed me over?" he asked pointedly.

"Yes," she said, willfully ignoring the emphasis he'd placed on family. She pulled her arm free. "I certainly understand why you're so angry."

"Oh, that's very generous of you."

"After all," she continued in a voice dripping with amiability. She strolled to the sofa and sat, as calmly as if they were discussing the weather. "My father treated you very badly."

"Your father?" he asked again, his indignation growing. She'd crushed his heart and now she thought he should be angry with her father? "You don't seriously think this is about how *your father* treated me."

"Of course it is." Her composure slipped a notch. She crossed and uncrossed her legs as if trying not to fidget. "You want revenge. That's only natural. Since he's not here, you're taking it out on me."

"That's priceless." He nearly laughed at her audacity. He stalked toward her, waiting for her to flinch, but she didn't. "Are you trying to deflect my anger or do you honestly believe that you're not responsible for what happened fourteen years ago?"

Apparently she could sit no longer. She stood, suddenly one hundred percent the defiant, rebellious Evie he'd once known. She bumped her chin up a notch and glared at him from across the tiny living room. "We had equal parts in what happened fourteen years ago. We're both to blame."

"Let me get this straight. You blame me?"

At the sound of Quinn's raised voice, the dog, who had slept through his arrival, lifted his head and blinked sleepily at him, before flopping back down on the floor.

Despite her confident tone, Evie frowned, as if—for only a second—she was baffled by his indignation. "I don't blame *only* you. That's my point. We're both responsible. And I think we'll both be better off if we talk about what happened."

"Well, I don't."

But she ignored him. "If we get it out in the open, maybe we can move on."

"Oh, I've moved on just fine." Except he hadn't. And the more she talked, the more he protested. And the more obvious it was that he was lying.

Exasperation flickered over her face, as if his interruption annoyed her. "If we can just admit the mistakes we both made—"

"The mistakes we *both* made?"

He'd made the mistake of trusting her. Of believing she could love him. Of loving her.

And now he'd made the additional mistake of letting himself get maneuvered into coming here. He never should have seen her in the first place. The humiliation of having his entire company know that he couldn't face his ex would have been vastly preferable to this mess.

"Is that really what you expected to happen tonight?"

He walked toward her, drawn to her, as he always had been. "You thought I'd come over, have a drink. Reminisce about the past."

She looked startled. "I wouldn't have used the word reminisce, but—"

"And what? That I'd just give you the fifty thousand dollars?"

"Well, I—" she protested.

He could see it in her eyes. That was what she'd thought would happen. She'd honestly expected him to just hand her the money.

"You must really think a lot of your conversational skills." Or, as was far more likely, she thought highly of her ability to manipulate and control him.

She seemed to flounder for a minute, looking as off-balanced as he felt. Then, with a shrug, she said, "It's more that I think we have a lot to talk about."

"But that isn't why I came here tonight. That's not what I agreed to pay you fifty thousand dollars for."

For a second, she hesitated and he thought he had her. He imagined he saw her struggling to keep her composure. Then she called his bluff, getting right in his face.

"What are you saying, Quinn? That you really came here tonight to have sex with me?"

"That was the plan," he said with grim acceptance. They were mere inches apart, him looking down at her, her glaring up at him. Tension oscillated between them. The air practically vibrated with it.

"The plan? I think threat is a better word."

"Don't try to make me the bad guy here." But even as he said it, he knew there was no other possible role for him to play. He was acting like a total jerk. He knew it and he didn't care.

What had she expected? Surely she hadn't thought he'd just sit and chat. Like they were at a freakin' tea party.

"What is it you want from me, Evie?" He grabbed her arms, wanting to shake her in his frustration. Instead, he felt the heat of her through her sweater. Her arms were small but strong. Like her. "Besides the money, I mean. You want me to grovel and beg for your affection? You want me to fall for you all over again? To become so completely enchanted by you that I forget how you screwed me over fourteen years ago?"

"Is that really what you think? That this was part of my plan to lure you in?" Shoving at his chest, she wrenched herself free from his grasp. "That in my elaborate plan to seduce you and make you fall for me all over again, I'm wearing my jeans and ratty sweater?"

She plucked at the hem of her sweater, full of false indignation. As if she were completely unaware of how appealing she looked. As if she hadn't picked her jeans because they hugged her hips and emphasized the narrow width of her waist. As if she didn't know that the moss-green sweater perfectly matched her eyes and that the soft knit clung to her breasts. That the casual disarray of her curls made him think of tousled sheets and lazy, early-morning sex.

Of course, maybe she really didn't know. Because

she kept on talking as if he wasn't seconds away from ripping her clothes off.

"Or perhaps you think it goes deeper than this? Maybe you think I've fabricated this whole situation? That my brother isn't really in danger. That I don't really need the money. That I thought making myself seem pathetic would appeal to you."

He struggled for a response but didn't come up with one. What could he possibly say that wouldn't reveal that—regardless of whether or not she'd planned it—he did want her. Despite himself, he craved her. He remembered exactly how she'd tasted. How she'd felt in his arms.

But he didn't want to want her. With every fiber of his being he wanted to hate her. And the fact that he didn't made him despise himself almost as much as he wanted to despise her.

His emotions must have shown through because after studying his face for a minute, she shook her head and spoke.

"Here's what I don't get. If you're this mad at me, if this is really just about humiliating me, then why choose this?" She spread out her hands to indicate their situation.

Playing dumb seemed the safest course of action, so he said, "I don't know what you mean."

"If retribution is what you want, there have got to be a hundred other ways to ground my dignity under your heel. So what could you possibly achieve by taking this route? If I'm so distasteful to you, why bring sex into this at all?"

"Is that what you think? That you're distasteful to me?"

"Well, it seems pretty apparent to me." Her anger crept into her voice. "Obviously you hate me. So why pretend you want to sleep with me?"

Of course, he couldn't admit the truth. That where she was concerned, his emotions were so raw he'd proposed to sleep with her just to get her out of his office.

Even when he knew she was manipulating him he wanted her. Even when she was using him to get money. He was still drawn to her. To her sheer bravado. To her wild streak of rebellion that she could never keep down for long.

And that was the fatal flaw in his plan. He'd thought to push her away with his arrogant, obnoxious behavior. With any other woman it might have worked. But he'd forgotten one thing. Evie was at her best when backed into a corner. She was at her loveliest when fighting— whether it was for a hopeless cause or in defense of someone she cared about. Right now, fighting him, she was every inch the girl who'd stolen his heart.

If he wasn't careful, he'd fall in love with her all over again. Hell, he'd be lucky if he got out of here without dropping to his knees and begging her for forgiveness.

She was looking at him expectantly, waiting for him to answer. Since he had to say something, he bluffed with a half lie. "Have you heard of Occam's razor?"

"Of course. The scientific principle that the simplest explanation is the most likely."

"Exactly." Because admitting he desired her physically was much easier—not to mention safer—than admitting the truth. That she appealed to him on every level. That he just wanted her. "The simplest explanation for why I entered this arrangement is because I desire you. I want you in my bed."

"But you don't even like me."

"I'm a man. I don't have to like you to find you physically attractive."

"Well, I'm a woman, and generally speaking, we aren't attracted to men we don't like. Which is just one more reason I'm not going to sleep with you."

Her eyes were filled with pure defiance and daring. He almost believed that she meant it. That the passion between them had been completely buried by the bitter emotions of the past.

But it hadn't been for him and he couldn't believe it had been for her. And he couldn't live with himself if he didn't figure out if she was bluffing, just as he was. And the only way he'd know the truth was to kiss her and find out.

She didn't really believe he was going to kiss her, until the instant his lips met hers. For a moment, she fought against the embrace. She didn't struggle. Didn't try to squirm out of his arm. Didn't demand he release her.

But she resisted it. Tried to maintain her emotional defenses. He wanted to kiss her? Fine. He wanted to humiliate her? Okay, maybe after all her family had done to him, maybe she had it coming.

However, she had no intention of letting it go further than this. She didn't believe for a minute that this had anything to do with sexual desire. His touch was too impersonal. His embrace too cold.

But then, in imperceptible increments, the kiss changed. His lips softened, his hands warmed, his body leaned into hers. She didn't see it coming. It happened before she could raise her defenses against it. Before she could do what she should have done before: end the kiss and put physical—not to mention emotional—distance between them.

The very air around them seemed to shimmer and shift. To vibrate with familiarity.

Suddenly, she wasn't kissing a cold-hearted stranger. That man disappeared. And in an instant she was kissing Quinn.

Quinn. Who she'd loved like she'd loved no one else. Who'd been the single bright spot throughout her very rough teenage years. Who'd always made her laugh. Who'd listened to her ideas. Who'd expected more of her than anyone else. Who'd made her stretch. Made her yearn.

For her, Quinn was youth and hope. He was strength and defiance. He spoke to the wildness of her soul. To the restless, untamed corners of her spirit.

With his lips moving over hers, with the scent of him in her nose, she felt sixteen again. Full of hope and lust for life. Thrilled with the pleasure humming through her veins. Giddy with the power to give as much pleasure as she received.

Lost in that memory, her whole being sank into the kiss. Her arms snaked up around his shoulders. And dang it, those really were his shoulders. No fancy padding lining his jacket. No flabby belly beneath his shirt. Just Quinn.

She shoved at the lapels of his jacket, working it off his shoulders. For an instant, he released her, allowing the coat to drop to the floor.

Despite herself, she relished Quinn's embrace and the feeling of his hands on her. Like she'd finally come home after years of being lost in the big wide world without him.

She wanted to go on kissing him forever. She wanted to spend hours—days even—exploring all of his body. She wanted to strip off her clothes and lose herself in mindless, pounding passion.

She threaded her fingers through his hair, deepening the kiss, plastering her body against his. Every cell of her skin prickled to his touch, but he kept his hands firmly on her shoulders. Then he took one step forward, edging her backward. And another. She felt the wall against her back providing leverage she used to buck her body against his. But she wanted more. She didn't just want to touch him, she wanted to crawl inside his skin. Burrow into the sanctuary of his soul and never leave.

Then, as abruptly as he'd started the kiss, he ended it. Wrenching her hands from him, he set her aside and stepped away from her.

"Well." He dragged his thumb across his lower lip as if wiping away her touch. "That was interesting."

She blinked, too shocked to do more.

"Obviously you're more attracted to me than you thought you were," he said.

He paused, appraising her coolly. Making her painfully aware of her rapid breathing. Of the heated blood thrumming through her body. Of the very pulse of her desire.

Slowly he turned away, his expression blank, his hands shoved deep into his pockets. "I, however, find that I'm not as willing to overlook your personality flaws as I thought I would be. Then again, maybe I lied. Maybe this really is about revenge. Because I find I can't make myself go through with this after all."

"Wait." She stepped forward, reaching out her hand but then dropping it to her side again. "Where are you going?"

"Home," he said simply, sweeping his jacket up and draping it over his arm. "I suddenly feel like I need a hot shower."

Watching him leave, her mind reeled. Perversely, only one coherent thought emerged from the chaos of her mind. "What about the money?" she asked.

He turned back, almost to the door. "That's right. This was supposed to be about money, wasn't it?" He looked her coolly up and down. "You haven't earned it."

Three

Evie recoiled as if slapped, but she snapped back quickly. "No. You're the one walking out. That means you're breaking our bargain. Not me."

He heard distress in her voice. Any savvy business-man knew to take advantage of that kind of desperation. Maybe she hoped he was too dense to hear it. Dense seemed to be his specialty these days.

Lucky for her, he wasn't in the mood to take advantage of her right now. He was far too disconcerted by his own display of weakness for that. Truth was, he had to get out of here before he did something really stupid, like beg her for forgiveness. It was one thing to admit to himself that he was acting like a total ass. Another thing entirely to admit it to anyone else. Let alone Evie.

She grabbed his arm just as he reached for the door. "There's got to be another way. You promised." Her tone was pleading, but it was her eyes—large and luminous—that really got to him.

What about the promises you made to me? he wanted to ask.

The promise to love him. To cherish him. To make a life with him. To grow old with him.

Yeah. That'd make him seem tough.

Instead, he looked her up and down. "That was when I thought you might be worthy fifty thousand dollars. I've changed my mind."

The image of her shocked face, of the tears pooling in her eyes, stayed with him all the way back to his condo. He feared it would be with him far longer. Because back at home, stretched out on his sleek leather sofa, staring mindlessly at whatever was playing on ESPN2, all he could think about was Evie.

He was haunted by what it had been like to kiss her again. In his arms, she hadn't felt like a conniving little tramp. She'd felt like the girl he'd once loved.

What if he was wrong about her? What if she wasn't to blame for what had happened all of those years ago? Worse still, what if she wasn't the manipulative little rich girl he'd imagined she was?

Seeing her house and how she lived made that scenario seem all too possible. He knew now how desperate her financial situation was. Before stepping foot in her house, he'd checked up on her finances. He'd known that she lived in that dumpy little house in that questionable neighborhood because she couldn't afford anywhere else. Nevertheless, he'd acted like a jerk.

Ever since she'd walked back into his life, he'd been doing his damnedest to push her out again. He'd been insulting and rude and she just kept coming back for more. This had to stop.

Frankly, he couldn't take much more of this. He was entirely too vulnerable to her. It would be bad enough if all he wanted was to sleep with her. But that was just the tip of the iceberg. He wanted to protect her. To sweep her away from the tawdriness of her everyday life. To whisk her away from her crime-infested neighborhood to some pristine suburban tract house.

This was bad.

He had to get her out of his life for good. And if that meant writing her a check for fifty grand, then so be it. He couldn't risk the possibility that she would come ask him for the money again. God only knew what he'd do the next time.

The view from the terrace of Corbin's uptown condo always took Evie's breath away. She often thought that if the state ever started paying social workers ten or twenty times what they made now, maybe she'd sell her shoe box in Oak Cliff and buy a loft like this. The air was surprisingly fresh and faintly scented with the rosemary Corbin kept in planters along the railing. The view of the historic Arts District and downtown beyond always soothed her. Up here, looking at the city from this distance, the flaws seemed to fade. Nothing was dirty or ugly. Nothing was spoiled.

She wasn't someone who romanticized people. But maybe the distance of time had lolled her into forgetting Quinn's bad qualities—that stubborn pride of his for starters—just as these seventeen floors blurred the less-appealing features of the street level.

She didn't know what to think of Quinn's behavior the previous evening. She didn't think of Quinn as a cruel person. But he'd been cruel last night. But not maliciously, even she could see that. No, his anger had been pure defensiveness.

Of course, that didn't excuse it. Thinking it was okay for someone in pain to be mean was a dangerous attitude. Even if you were in pain, it wasn't okay to hurt others. Still, it saddened her to think he'd held on to so much resentment. There was nothing she could do about it, though. She had bigger problems to deal with. More immediate at least.

Just then, Corbin came out onto the terrace with his cup of coffee in hand, the tension vibrating off of him disrupting the brief illusion that this was just another one of their lazy Saturday-morning brunches.

"I've never understood how you could afford to live here," she said. "Given your current financial crisis, maybe you should consider moving somewhere a little more within your price range."

Corbin's smile was tinged with bitterness. "No lectures today, sis."

"Fair enough. First we deal with the gun-toting bad

guys that want your appendages, then we'll tackle the concept of living within one's means."

For an instant, Corbin looked as if he wanted to smile, but then his face twisted into that wounded puppy dog look of his. "How can you joke at a time like this?"

How can I not? she wanted to ask. "You were a lot more fun before you owed money to scary men."

His frown deepened.

She held up her hands in a display of innocence. "Okay, I'll stop. But I can't help it. Gallows humor is a professional hazard for social workers, you know."

Which was true—most social workers, herself included, used humor to diffuse the dehumanizing problems they dealt with at work. Right now, about the only way she could talk about Corbin's situation was with humor. Anything else made her want to burst into tears.

She swallowed the last of her coffee and set the mug aside, twisting in her seat so she faced Corbin instead of the view.

Because Corbin seemed so disheartened—and who could blame him?—she gave him what she hoped was a reassuring pat on the hand. "We'll find a solution. Don't worry."

Corbin smiled wanly. "I know. You're such a big sister."

She chuckled. "Boy, that's classic."

"What?" he asked, all innocence.

"You managed to criticize me even when you're relying on my help."

"I wasn't—"

"Yes, you were," she said. "You think I meddle."

"You *do* meddle," he quipped, before taking a slurp of his coffee. "Half the time you treat me like I'm one of your lame pets you've brought home from the animal shelter."

She didn't bother to point out that half the time he acted less responsible than her pets, who at least had the decency to clean up after themselves and occasionally contribute to the household by catching lizards.

"And yet," she pointed out, "no matter how annoyed you are with my meddling, you'll still accept my help, won't you?"

"It's not that your meddling annoys me, sis. I just wish you had more going on in your life than taking care of me and the other misfits. I might not always be around, you know."

Any response she might have made caught in her throat at his open reference to the danger he was in. For a moment, his glib cynicism wavered and a spark of real affection shown in his eyes. She could almost imagine they were kids once more. That he was the baby brother who'd looked up to her no matter what.

"I do appreciate it, you know," he said with a quirk to his lips. "You going to this party tonight so you can talk to Quinn for me."

"About that…" She hesitated, feeling an unnatural spike of guilt for going behind Corbin's back.

What did she have to feel guilty about? Corbin had bought a ticket for her for tonight's big Diamonds in the Rough charity fundraiser. It was an annual silent auction held at Messina Diamonds. Even though it was a charity she believed in, one that sponsored troubled teens at a summer leadership camp, she'd never dream of attending on her own. Partly because she'd never be able to justify the cost of the tickets, but mostly because she'd never risk running into Quinn.

When Corbin had first asked her to approach Quinn about the money, he'd presented her with a ticket to the event so she could use that opportunity to get Quinn alone. However, she'd decided on her own to attend the fundraiser only as a last resort.

"About that," she began. "After we talked, I decided going to the fundraiser was a bad idea."

Corbin's head spun around and he gave her a piercing look.

"I know Quinn better than you do. I didn't think he'd react well to being put on the spot like that. So I made an appointment and talked to him beforehand."

"We agreed you'd go to the fundraiser."

There was a hard note to Corbin's voice that she'd never heard before. It was unlike her erratic brother to be so firm about anything.

"I know that's what we talked about. But the element of surprise would not have worked in our favor at any rate. He was…" she searched her mind for the right word to describe his response "…difficult enough as it was."

"What do you mean 'difficult'?"

"He said no." Then she rushed to reassure Corbin, leaving out all the more unpleasant aspects of that "no."

"But we'll figure something out. I'll talk to Dad again. Or maybe Uncle Vernon. We haven't talked to him in years."

She let her words trail off, since Corbin was waving them aside anyway. And was that relief she saw in his eyes? Was he just glad she was willing to do so much on his behalf, or was there something else going on here?

"No, you still have to go tonight. Just talk to him again," he said.

"I'm not going to do that."

"You have to."

"Corbin, you're not listening. He was quite insistent. He's not going to give us the money."

But Corbin ignored her protestations. "Wait till you see what I bought for you." He jumped up from his seat.

Curious about his burst of energy and his attitude, she followed. She found him in the bedroom, pulling a full-length evening gown from his closet.

"I bought this for you to wear to the party." He pulled off the plastic store bag and spread the gown on his bed.

The dress was a brilliant teal silk, shot through with silver threads so it shimmered as it moved. The bodice was an off-center halter that managed to look both elegant and unexpected. The dress flared out at the hips. The bottom third of the dress was etched with a scrawled batik pattern, giving the overall dress a hint of the exotic. She'd never seen—let alone worn—anything like it.

"Oh, Corbin," she murmured. Unable to resist the urge, she reached out to rub the hem of the dress between her thumb and forefinger. "You stupid, stupid man."

"What?"

"This must have cost a fortune."

He shrugged. "It wasn't that much."

He said it with such innocence she almost believed him. "You can't snow me, Corbin. I haven't always been poor. Don't forget, before Mom died she used to take me shopping in Dallas."

Though Dallas was hours away from their hometown, it was where all of Mason's elite went to shop. Not that she'd ever had occasion to buy something like that with her mom, who'd died before Evie made it to high school, let alone homecoming or prom. Still, she could remember sitting on the dressing room floor as her mother tried on clothes like this. Beautiful, decadent fantasies of clothing. Dresses spun of fairy magic and wealth.

"Don't insult my intelligence by pretending I don't know what a dress like this would cost."

"I know the designer," Corbin hedged. "He let me have it at cost."

"And it still probably cost ten times more than either one of us has. Even if I was going to go—which I'm not—I wouldn't wear this. I have a perfectly acceptable dress at home."

Corbin stared at her blankly for a minute before a look of profound distaste settled on his face. "The red one?"

"It's burgundy, but yes, that's the one I was planning on wearing. It's a nice dress."

"You've worn it to every Christmas party for the past eight years."

"Six," she protested. "And that wine stain is hardly noticeable."

"You'll look like a social worker." Corbin infused the words *social worker* with roughly the same inflection he would use to say *sewage treatment engineer*.

"I *am* a social worker."

"But you don't want to look like one. Not in a room full of Dallas's wealthiest and most beautiful. You'll never get his attention that way. Besides, you don't have the burgundy dress anymore."

"Of course I—"

"I got rid of it."

"You what?" If it had been anyone else, she wouldn't have believed him capable. But in his own way, Corbin was as bossy as she was. Throwing out her dress so she'd have to wear the one he'd picked out was exactly the sort of childish thing he'd do. "When?"

"Last week while you were out."

"While I was out? You mean while I was at work. Or possibly even when I was out begging for money for you."

Corbin just rolled his eyes. Of course, he'd never begged for anything in his life. He had no idea how humiliating it was. Particularly when you ended up kissing someone you had no right being attracted to. In that light, her brother getting rid of the admittedly ugly burgundy dress was the least of her worries.

"It doesn't matter," she said. "I'm not going tonight."

"You have to go." Corbin waved a hand over the teal dress. "And in this, he'll notice you. You'll look gorgeous."

For the briefest instant an image flashed through her

mind of what it would be like to walk into the party tonight dressed in this beautiful gown. Oh, it had been so long since she'd worn something this lovely. Since she'd dressed with the intention of turning a man's head.

She didn't have a job that valued being pretty. Ergo, she had no clothes in which she felt outrageously gorgeous. She itched to put it on. To feel the silk shimmer and slide beneath her fingers. To feel the weight of it sway against her legs.

To feel the weight of Quinn's attention as she walked into the room. Sure, he hadn't wanted her in jeans and an old sweater, but she'd like to see him walk away from her while she was wearing this dress.

Whoa, hang on there, Sparky. You're not going to the party. You're not wearing the dress. You're certainly not trying to snag Quinn's attention.

She raised an accusing pointer finger at Corbin. "Stop trying to distract me. It doesn't matter how I'll look. He's not going to give me the money."

"He loved you, Evie. And when he sees you in this—"

"But he doesn't love me now. He doesn't even like me. He's not going to give me the money just because I'm wearing a pretty dress."

"Evie," Corbin chided. "This isn't just a pretty dress. This is a knock-his-socks-off dress. He has to see you in this."

"But—"

"Just promise me you'll go." Corbin snatched at her hands and held them tight within his own. "Just talk to him again. Promise me."

His palms were sweaty against hers. His tone desperate, his eyes pleading.

"Corbin, what is wrong?"

"Nothing. I mean, beside the gun-toting bad guys who want my appendages." His smile was overly bright. "Stay here and commune with the dress. I'm going to get you another cup of coffee."

"No, I've already had—" But he'd disappeared around the corner before she could get out the words "too much caffeine."

What was she going to do with him? His life was in danger and here he was making her coffee and buying her expensive clothes. At times he seemed to have no common sense. He lived well beyond his means and yet didn't seem aware of what his means even were.

She surveyed his bedroom. When he'd moved in, he'd had the place professionally decorated in the sleek modern style he preferred. The condo had been a show-place, but he lived like a slob. He never even made his bed.

Out of habit and to avoid looking at the dress—lest it stir any more images in her mind of bringing Quinn to his knees—she wandered around the room, scooping up clothes to toss in the wicker hamper that sat unused in the corner. Then she quickly made the bed. She found one pillow down at the footboard, the other on the floor on the far side of the bed.

When she picked up the pillow, she noticed something sticking out from under the bed. A set of blueprints.

She stared in confusion at the thick sheaf of papers. Corbin had a lot of interests, but architecture had never been one of them. The plans lay flat, unrolled with some of the pages folded back over the set to reveal a page in the middle. The words Messina Diamonds were printed across the top of the page.

She flipped from one page to the next, dread growing in her belly. There were multiple pages for each of the six floors that Messina Diamonds occupied in their downtown building. Floor plans, design specs and electrical information. There was also page after page of information about the building in general. Pages for McCain Security and for other businesses she didn't recognize the names of.

She heard Corbin out in the hall and instinctively shoved everything back under the bed. She straightened just as he entered with the fresh mug of coffee.

"What are you doing?" His tone was sharp with caution.

"Just looking for your pillows," she said quickly. "You know me, I can't help but pick up after you."

But as she accepted the mug of coffee and allowed Corbin to lead her back out to the patio, her mind was racing and her dread multiplying like gnats. What mess had he gotten himself into this time? Why on earth would someone need architectural plans for a company they had nothing to do with? If he had any legitimate reason for having them, why keep them under his bed? The only conclusion she could reach was that whatever Corbin was involved with, this time she wouldn't be able to pick up after him.

An hour later, as she watched Corbin hanging the

dress in the back of her aging Civic, she realized something else. This morning, Corbin hadn't once asked her to get the money from Quinn. He'd said things like "talk to him" and "get his attention." He hadn't actually mentioned getting the money from Quinn.

Did that mean Corbin had another way to get the money he needed? A way that involved her seeing Quinn tonight? More specifically, her seeing Quinn while wearing a knock-his-socks-off dress?

Hmmm, a plan that involved a fundraiser at a diamond company, a woman in a pretty dress and a distracted guy in charge of security. Maybe she'd been watching those Ocean's movies too many times, but this was not adding up well.

Whatever Corbin was planning, he was using her as a distraction. And this fancy dress was just bait.

Was she right or was she just being paranoid? She needed a second opinion. She needed to tell Quinn.

Dang it. The only way she had to get in touch with Quinn was via his work phone number. Before contacting him for the first meeting, she'd exhausted all her resources looking for a personal number but had not found one. And since McCain Security's business office was undoubtedly closed on a Saturday afternoon, that left only one option. She was going to have to go to that fundraiser after all. And she would have to wear the beautiful dress because frankly, nothing else in her closet came even close to being appropriate for the event.

She would look smashing. More to the point, she would look as though she was *trying* to look smashing.

As if she was trying to win him back. On the bright side, he wouldn't really believe that. Not for long anyway. Not once she told him her brother was planning to rob Messina Diamonds.

Four

Friday night should have been the last time he ever had to be in the same room as Evie. And, in fact, it probably would have been if he hadn't waffled so long over the damn check.

Instead, he had signed the check and left it sitting on the corner of his desk for the better part of the morning. Ostensibly he was waiting to shuffle some money around, just to be sure. Even he wasn't used to writing checks this big on a whim. The possibility that he might be waiting for some sign from her was ridiculous. Not really worth considering.

Nevertheless, by the time Quinn had dressed for the Diamonds in the Rough event at Messina Diamonds that night, he still hadn't had the check sent over to Evie.

Quinn had never been comfortable with these kind of high-society events. He attended them only because Messina Diamonds was his biggest client. He didn't handle the account himself anymore—he'd long ago turned those duties over to J.D. Roker, his very competent second in command. His friendship with Derek alone wouldn't have been enough to coax him into a tux. However, no matter how much he trusted Roker, he still wanted to be on hand whenever the company's office was open to the public.

Still, when he ran into Raina in the Messina Diamonds' foyer that night, he found himself wishing he was a less vigilant CEO. Raina had long been Derek's secretary and they'd married just a few months ago. Though they now lived most of the year in Poughkeepsie, where Raina was attending culinary school, they'd been in Dallas all week preparing for the event. Diamonds in the Rough was one of Raina's pet projects back from the days when she'd worked as Derek's secretary.

Quinn arrived at the Messina Diamond offices to find the caterer setting up and the florist arranging displays throughout the offices. The charity's volunteers had long ago organized the various items that had been donated for the silent auction. And Raina was bustling around overseeing it all.

He smiled when he saw her. "You know there's not much for you to do, right? It's all been taken care of ahead of time."

She crossed the room to give him a kiss on the cheek.

"I know. But it's the first time I haven't been here to supervise everything myself."

"It'll be perfect. You know it will. You should just let it go and enjoy the evening for once."

"Hmm, that sounds to me like a case of the pot calling the kettle black." She flashed him a knowing smile. "After all, it's not like you're going to leave all of the security to the very capable J.D. and just let it go and enjoy the evening."

He nodded. "Good point."

"Speaking of enjoying the evening…" Raina bit her lip as if unsure how to proceed. Which was unlike her. Normally Raina was as straight-talking as they came.

"Spit it out." Her hesitancy made him nervous and he fought the urge to tug at his sleeves, straighten his tie or some other little foible that would reveal too much of his emotion.

"Have you seen the guest list?"

"Not for a couple of weeks. J.D.'s been handling all the details for tonight. Part of that whole 'relaxing and letting go' thing we were talking about."

"She's coming tonight."

Ah, crap. "By 'she,' can I assume you mean Evie?"

Raina nodded.

"I suppose I have Derek to thank for this?"

"For me knowing who Evie is? Actually, no. Derek hasn't said a word about her. But, for most people, the former Mrs. McCain is the most interesting bit of gossip since…well, for a long time."

Pink crept into Raina's cheeks. So he could only

assume that "for a long time" meant since Derek had found out he was a father and then Raina—inadvertently—had broken up Derek's engagement to jewelry store heiress Kitty Biedermann. At the time he'd felt sorry for Derek, knowing the other man must hate being the focus of his employees' gossip. And now he found himself in a similar position. Great.

"You're being unnaturally quiet," Raina commented. "Even for you."

He smiled, hoping the action came off as amused and not simply terrified. "I'm trying to avoid thinking about it."

Which, if the expression on Raina's face was any indication, he should not have admitted. She reached out and gave his arm an empathetic squeeze.

"Don't worry. I'll have her tossed out the minute she shows up. You won't even have to see her."

"That's not neces—"

A light of fierce protectiveness lit her eyes. "I'll make sure she knows she's not welcome here."

Great. Just what he needed. The delicate Raina going into battle for him. That would show everyone.

"Raina," he began, his tone a steely warning. "I don't want you to talk to her. I don't care if she's here tonight."

Raina frowned. "Of course you care. She's your ex-wife." Before he could protest more, she pointed out, "Besides, if you really didn't care, then you wouldn't have gone stone still the moment I mentioned her."

He wanted to argue the point, but it was a moot one anyway. A moment later, his cell phone buzzed, ending the conversation. He was glad for the interruption until he answered the call from J.D., who was down on the ground floor preparing to check invitations for the guests who would start arriving any minute now.

"There's a woman here who claims she needs to see you right away."

Through sheer force of will alone, Quinn didn't curse. "I assume it's Evie Montgomery."

J.D. paused just long enough to confirm Quinn's suspicions. "Affirmative."

And now even his employees were walking on eggshells around him. This was exactly the kind of crap he'd wanted to avoid.

"Escort her up to my office."

He might as well get this over with. The night—which hadn't promised to be a pleasant evening anyway—had been going steadily downhill. Wasn't it bad enough that he'd had to see her last night? He'd had the joy of having her poke and prod at his emotions.

After all these years, he was doubting himself. And if that wasn't bad enough, now he was going to be haunted by yet another memory of what she felt like in his arms. By the taste of her mouth beneath his. And now, on top of all of that, he had to face her again? Fine. Bring it on. Things couldn't get any worse.

Five minutes later, when J.D. showed Evie into Quinn's office, he wished he'd been a little more careful in his predictions of the future.

She looked as though she'd been poured into a shimmering teal dress. Her ivory skin gleamed, her auburn hair fell in loose tumbling waves. The fact that she looked ill at ease in the dress only added to her appeal. Every cell in his body leapt in response to the sight of her.

Yep. Things could get worse. A whole lot worse.

If she had thought—even for a moment—that her past relationship with Quinn might make it easier to admit to him that she suspected her brother was about to rob Messina Diamonds, the instant she saw Quinn, she realized how mistaken she'd been.

This man, dressed in a crisply elegant tux, with his cool, assessing gaze and his unreadable expression, could have been a complete stranger. Except she had the added humiliation of knowing that last night, when he'd kissed her, she'd responded. She'd actually wanted him. And he hadn't wanted her.

Now, standing in his office, she could almost believe that he didn't remember her from twenty-four hours ago, let alone from fourteen years ago.

Maybe she should have gone to the police.

But they probably wouldn't have believed her anyway. And Quinn, at least, was in a position to stop Corbin before it was too late. Before Corbin crossed the line into outright criminal behavior.

"I need your help," she began unceremoniously.

"We already had this conversation."

Ah, so he did remember coming to her house and kissing her senseless.

"Yes, we did. But I need something else from you."

"I've already written the check," he said, settling

himself behind the massive desk. "I was going to have it couriered over to you on Monday."

He said the words with a sort of detached casualness. As if he wasn't talking about fifty thousand dollars. As if just last night he hadn't told her she wasn't worth the money.

So he had just been toying with her.

Great. Well, then he would love having this new opportunity to torture her.

"It's not about the money. Or maybe it is." Dang it, this would be *so* much easier if she hadn't let him kiss her last night. What had she been thinking? Besides, *Oh, baby, baby, take my clothes off?* "The thing is, I don't think Corbin really wanted me to ask you for the money. I think he's planning on stealing it."

Quinn's eyebrows shot up. After a moment, he rocked back in his chair. "So why come to me?"

"I think he's planning on stealing it from Messina Diamonds."

For a second, he looked as shocked as she felt. Then—much to her consternation—he threw his head back and laughed.

She frowned. And then frowned more when his laughter subsided very slowly. She even found herself drumming her fingers against her leg, waiting for him to stop.

"My brother—"

"Couldn't steal a pen from the receptionist without me knowing it."

"I'm not joking," she insisted.

Quinn's smile faded, and he leaned forward in his chair, propping his elbows on his desk. After a long moment, he said, "This is a either a bad joke—"

"It's not."

"Or another one of your attempts to screw with me."

It took a second for his words to register, but when they did, she shot out of her chair. "Is that what you think? Seriously? That all of this—" she gestured broadly to encompass the events of the past few days "—was nothing more than some elaborate plan to 'screw with you'?" She made sarcastic air quotes as she spoke. "I didn't come here just to help my brother. I came here to help you, too. And if you're too stubborn—no, too stupid—to see that, then you deserve whatever fallout you get when your biggest client is robbed right under your nose."

When it came to Evie, he had no judgment at all. So there was no point in pretending it went against his better judgment to stop her. He did it anyway. She was almost out his office door when he grabbed her arm.

"Hold up a minute, Evie. Why don't you tell me what's going on?"

Her gaze was filled with suspicion, but the light of anger in her eyes was all too reminiscent of the passion he'd seen in her just last night. He was probably going to regret this. Hell, he already regretted it. But if she was right and he let her walk out of here, it'd be an even bigger mistake.

"You'll listen to me?" she asked.

"I will."

"No sarcastic comments or snide suspicions?"

"If you expect some kind of declaration of trust—" he began.

"I was at Corbin's condo today and found a set of floor plans for Messina Diamonds' office." She said the words in a rush and then seemed to hold her breath, waiting for his response.

He studied her face, looking for signs she was lying. Trying not to notice the plump temptation of her lips. The way her chest rose and fell as nerves made her heart rate pick up.

"A copy of the blueprints?" he asked.

"Yes." She tugged her arm free, then rubbed the spot where he'd held her. "Why else would he have the blueprints unless he was planning to break in?"

Part of him was convinced she was lying to him. That this was just another one of her twisted games. But that same part of him—if asked last week—would have guessed that she'd married some rich guy her father had picked out for her and was now cruising around east Texas in her BMW going to junior league luncheons. Which meant there was a good chance that the part of him that was automatically suspicious of Evie was just misguided.

What if she was right? Was he really willing to take that risk?

Quinn scratched his jaw thoughtfully, then gestured to the chair for her to sit down. If they continued to stand there, mere inches apart, his baser instincts might get the better of him. "You'd better start from the beginning."

"I don't know much. I didn't want to confront him about it. I knew he would just deny everything. But I think that when he found out I was going to ask you for the money, he must have told the Mendoza brothers about my connection to you."

She sat perched on the edge of her chair, all restless energy and raw nerves. "A few weeks ago, when I first found out he owed money to the Mendoza brothers, I offered to come to you for money. At first he didn't want me to ask you. But he came up with this idea of me approaching you tonight. During the fundraiser. It's like he became obsessed with it. He bought me this ridiculous dress. I think I'm supposed to distract you tonight."

She chuckled uneasily. As if worried he might scoff at the idea that she could distract him.

Did she really not know how she looked in that dress? How tempting she was? Because Corbin really knew his stuff. Quinn could hardly think when she was in the room. He was saved from having to comment when she continued her story.

"I love my brother," she said with an exasperated sigh. "But I'm the first person to admit he can be an idiot. He's the stupidest smart person I know. It would be just like him to spout off to the wrong person that he had an 'in' with Messina Diamonds. Before he'd know it, these criminals he's been dealing with would have him backed into a corner and he'd have no idea how to get out of it." She nibbled on her lips, sending him a cautious look. "Do you think I'm crazy?"

"I think you've always had an excellent imagination."

"But I know my brother. And I know something is up."

"You think he's planning on stealing…" He let his words trail off, giving her the opportunity to fill in the blank.

"Diamonds, I assume."

"And why would you assume that?"

She shrugged. "Because this is a diamond mining company. It just seemed logical."

"It isn't. The diamonds are mined in Canada. They're cut at the Messina facility in Antwerp and then shipped directly to New York where they're sold on the market there. This office is primarily used for research and exploration as well as being the business headquarters. In fact, diamonds rarely make it here."

"Rarely?" she asked. "Rarely, but not never?"

"No. Not never. There's a safe in Derek's office. He does occasionally keep stones there."

"Are there any there now?"

He scrubbed a hand along the back of his neck. "No."

But apparently he'd hesitated just long enough to convince her there must be because she quirked an eyebrow. "Do you think I can't tell when you're lying to me?"

Quinn ignored her comment. "You seem pretty sure you know what he's planning."

"Well, I'm not. But I can't think of any other explanation. Can you?"

Now it was her turn to pin him with a stare. He had to stifle the urge to squirm. There were plenty of things he didn't want her reading in his expression. Things that had nothing to do with her brother or diamonds. "No. I can't. But it would be virtually impossible for Corbin to break into Messina Diamonds. They have the best system on the market."

As if she couldn't sit still any longer, she popped out of her chair and paced, etching out a circuitous path around leather wingback chairs. "Trust me," she said. "I don't want to be right about this. But neither of us can afford to be wrong, either."

"Neither of us?"

"Obviously. My brother's future is at risk, but for you the stakes are even higher right? This is your business." She pointed her index finger at him, punctuating her words with a jab. "The company you built with your own hands, so to speak. The last thing you want is for there to be some kind of a…" she fished around for the word before landing on the perfect one "…some kind of a heist at Messina Diamonds. They're your biggest client. If you can't protect them, that won't look very good, now will it?"

Unfortunately, she was right. As much as he'd love to boot her out to the curb and never see her again, he simply couldn't risk it. For the sake of his personal honor and his professional reputation, he had to guarantee that Corbin Montgomery didn't get his sticky fingers on a single piece of Messina Diamonds' property. And until Quinn did make sure, he was stuck with Evie. And her damn dress.

Which, he consoled himself, was slightly better than being stuck with Evie in no dress at all.

He leaned forward in his chair. "Sit down before you make yourself dizzy. And tell me everything you know."

Evie's triumph was short-lived. At least Quinn was listening to her. But she could celebrate that when this was all over with and her brother was safely back home, sans stolen goods.

"Only what I've told you so far. I gather I'm supposed to distract you. So whatever it is must be planned for tonight. And it must be here."

"You're sure it's going to happen at Messina Diamonds?"

"Yes." But then she corrected herself. "No. I'm not. The blueprints were open to the pages for Messina Diamonds, but they were several inches thick. They must have been for the whole building." Why hadn't she thought of that before? "Which means, maybe it's not the diamonds. Maybe there's some other target. The proceeds from tonight's event, maybe."

"It's a silent auction. All the transactions will take place later via credit card."

"What about other businesses in the building? Messina Diamonds is only a few floors, right?"

"It's six. McCain Security is another four. Twelve through fourteen are the business headquarters. The second floor is security for this building."

"So that's nearly twenty floors of other businesses that could be at risk."

Abruptly, Quinn stood. "All right then. Let's get going."

Confused from the sudden shift in conversation, she responded with a rather inelegant "Huh?" As she stood to follow him, she tacked on, "Where are we going?"

"First we're going to find J.D., who's heading up the security for tonight's event."

"And second?" she asked as she followed him out of his office to the bank of elevators.

"Then I'll come back here and check on the other businesses, floor by floor. If your brother is going to break in tonight, I'm going to find him and stop him."

"Great. I'll come with you."

He stilled in his tracks. "No."

She stopped short to keep from bumping into him. "Of course I'm coming."

"Absolutely not. Only building personnel with security-level clearance and McCain Security employees are allowed access to the security systems."

She grinned gamely. "Will I be vaporized on the spot?"

"This isn't a laughing matter."

"I didn't think it was. You don't see me laughing, do you? This is my brother's life that's at stake."

"That doesn't matter. We have security protocols for a reason."

"Yes, but you're the CEO. You can break the rules every once in a while. And unless you're planning on physically restraining me, you're stuck with me."

He looked tempted. But he simply muttered, "Come on, then. We've got a lot of work to do."

"But what about Messina Diamonds?"

"That's where J.D. comes in. He'll have enough men on staff to handle anything that happens there. We'll handle anything else."

Warmth coursed through her at his words. *We'll handle anything else.* She realized suddenly how much she'd missed that. The feeling of the two of them together facing down the world. That's how it had been when they were teenagers. How she'd thought it would always be. Before everything went so horribly wrong.

To hide the pure yearning his words stirred, she asked, "What about the party?"

"I didn't want to go anyway, did you?"

As the elevator carried them up to the Diamonds in the Rough gala, she realized something. This business with Corbin had finally broken through Quinn's icy reserve. He was no longer treating her like a complete stranger. It was a small consolation, not to mention probably temporary. If, God forbid, her brother was involved in this mess, then Quinn would have a whole new reason to hate her.

Five

J.D.—being a mere employee and not the CEO of McCain Security—didn't have the luxury of being able to laugh out loud when presented with the possibility that Messina Diamonds might be robbed. However, his lips twitched as he stood with his legs braced apart and his arms crossed over his chest and said simply, "Impossible."

"That's what I told her," Quinn supplied.

"But—"

"There's no 'but' about it." Then J.D. nodded respectfully. "With all due respect, ma'am."

Evie was about to snap back with a "don't you 'ma'am' me!" but before she could, J.D. popped a bubble in his gum with symbolic finality. He grinned with relish as he did it, giving her the impression he actually hoped someone did try it. However, since the someone in question was her flesh and blood, Evie couldn't be quite so optimistic about the prospect.

Quinn nodded his thanks, then added, "J.D., call in anyone extra we've got anyway. Just to be sure."

"Will do, boss."

J.D. turned away, pulling his cell phone out of his pocket as Quinn placed a hand on Evie's elbow and led her deeper into the maze of hallways that were the Messina Diamonds offices. By now the event was gearing up. The lobby was beginning to fill with tuxedoed men and bejeweled women. Waiters drifted through the crowd bearing trays of champagne-filled glasses and tiny artistically embellished appetizers.

"Feel better?" Quinn asked.

"Frankly, I won't feel better until this is all over with. I guess I should just be thankful that Messina Diamonds is okay, but that doesn't mean that Corbin isn't up to something. Or that he won't be caught by the police."

"You'll be able to relax after we check out the other businesses in the building," he said as he guided her toward the elevator bay.

"Yes, I will." For the first time all day, her tension eased up.

Since they were the only ones going down, they had the elevator to themselves for three floors. The weight of the silence broke her down after just a few seconds.

"About last night—" she began.

He didn't let her finish. "I'd rather not talk about last night." With his hands buried in his pockets and without quite meeting her gaze, he said, "My behavior yesterday was uncalled for."

"Is that an apology?" she teased before she thought better of it. When he scowled, she added hastily, "No, don't answer. I'll assume it was and that your intentions were good without you having to confirm or deny it." Then she added in a more serious tone, "Yes, yesterday you acted like a total jerk. Whether or not it was warranted is a moot point. But today…" She shrugged. "Well, I'm not saying you've redeemed yourself exactly. But today you've made good strides. Thank you for taking me seriously."

Before he could respond, the elevator doors slid open to reveal the twelfth floor. She left the elevator and found herself facing the frosted glass doors etched with the name McCain Security. The same doors she'd faced just a few days before. Before she could contemplate how much had changed in so little time, the elevator doors chimed shut behind Quinn.

"Don't make the mistake of misinterpreting my generosity."

"Oh, I'm sorry. Did my teasing hurt your feelings?"

He scowled at her. "My feelings have nothing to do with this."

"Oookay," she agreed verbally, if not intellectually. "You behaved badly. You admit that. Why cut me a check afterward unless you intended it to be an apology? You must have *felt* some guilt."

He ignored the emphasis she'd put on the word "felt." Stepping back from her—since his stance had so obviously been another indication of his emotions—he tugged on the hem of his tux jacket and said, "Guilt had nothing to do with it. You were desperate and I took advantage of that. My behavior was…" obviously he had to search for a word that didn't imply guilt "…dishonorable."

Honor had always been a priority for him. Unlike other teenage boys she'd known, who never gave such things a second thought, he'd had his own code of ethics, even at seventeen. The world and fate had treated him badly. Guarding his own honor had been his only defense against injustice. That fierce sense of right and wrong was one of the things she'd loved best about him.

"I'm glad you still care about things like that," she mused aloud.

He sent her a piercing look. "Despite my recent behavior, I'm not a monster."

"I didn't say you were." She'd thought his behavior was less monstrous and more wounded. But of course the last time she'd suggested that, he'd responded by propositioning her. So this time around she kept her mouth shut.

It took a great deal of willpower on her part not to point out that he must have felt guilty—or perhaps ashamed of himself—for behaving in a way he saw as dishonorable.

If she'd expected him to say more, she'd have been disappointed. He merely made a noncommittal grunting noise, as he pulled his ID tag from his pocket and swiped it over the pad to the right of the glass door.

With a faint "swooshing" sound, the door latch released, and with a gallant sweep of his arm he gestured
for her to enter.

"So you can get into any office in the building?" she
asked.

"Pretty much."

She followed him through the reception area and
down the hall to an office just past the one she'd met
him in the other day. This office was more utilitarian
than his had been, with a bank of computers lining one
wall and a couple of office chairs. "I appreciate you
taking the time to check on this."

"This is my job. I'm not doing it for you." He sat
himself down in front of one of the computer monitors
and jiggled the mouse to wake up the computer.

She lowered herself to the spare chair. "Good point.
Still, I know this can't be easy for you."

"What's that supposed to mean?" He shot her a look
over his shoulder.

"Just that you'd probably rather be doing something
else. Given how you feel about me."

"I don't feel anything for you," he said blankly.
"You're nothing to me."

She should have let it go. She really should have. But
as the computer whirled to life in front of them, she
found herself saying, "No, I'm not. We were in love, for
goodness' sake. We were married. That's not nothing."

"You mean nothing to me," he repeated more slowly.

"Don't talk to me like that."

"Like what?" he asked innocently.

"Like that. As if I'm the one acting like an idiot, not you."

"I'm not—" But she didn't let him defend himself.

"A couple of years ago, I ran into an old college boyfriend. We went for coffee at Starbucks. He showed me pictures of his kids."

"Do you have a point?" he practically growled.

"My point is this. To him, I mean nothing. And you know how I know?"

Quinn slanted a look at her. "No."

"That right there." She waggled her finger in the direction of his face. "I know Jake doesn't care about me anymore because he never once looked at me like that."

"Like what?" he asked in a beleaguered voice.

"Like half the time you're wishing you could strangle me and the other half you're trying to figure out where you'd hide the body if you did."

"That's not what I'm thinking." As he said the words, he gave her a searing look. A sort of, I-want-you-naked-now look, as if he could peal off her clothes with pure telekinetic power. Her skin prickled as her body was flooded with molten heat.

"That is not the look of a man emotionally uninvolved," she said.

"Just drop it."

She rolled her eyes in exaggerated exasperation. "Oh, I'm sorry. Is this conversation getting too personal for you? Am I stepping all over those feelings you swear you don't have for me?"

"Leave it alone, Evie."

And with that, she heard the pain pinned beneath his words. There was a faint tremor in his voice. No, nothing as strong as a tremor. Just the faintest bit of huskiness that told her the words had been hard for him to say. His voice used to have that quality when he talked about his father. *"No, Ms. Gosling,"* he'd say, *"I didn't get the permission slip signed. My father wasn't able to sign it last night."* And everyone in the class would know that "not able to sign it" really meant "too drunk to hold a pen" and "last night" really meant "every night."

And he'd state it with the kind of casual blandness that let everyone ignore the truth. There they'd sit, a classroom full of people all too eager to ignore the fact that Quinn was neglected to the point of abuse. Quinn sitting there, praying no would call him on his lie, and her sitting beside him, wishing she could rail against the injustice of it.

Of course, only she knew him well enough to hear the anguish in his voice. That almost inaudible flicker of emotion. She heard it now when he said her name. And her heart broke all over again.

Before she could stop herself, she reached out and put her hand on his arm. "You always were too damn proud."

Time seemed to freeze, the moment telescoping, so that the whole world narrowed down to just the two of them. It was as if they were just kids again.

Then he broke eye contact and did something or other on the computer. "Let's just drop it."

His rebuff stung more than it should have. Damn it, she didn't want to get sucked back in to caring for him. That was so not part of her plan. To hide her vulnerability, she teased him. "Oh, have I hurt your feelings again?"

"No, just drop it because I just noticed that the camera is out on the eleventh floor."

"One of the cameras is out?" She sounded breathless with fear. "Then something is happening."

"Not necessarily," he said to reassure her, though his own internal alarm was jangling.

He pulled out his phone and dialed the extension for the second-floor office. The guard who should have been stationed there didn't pick up.

Quinn clicked the mouse a couple of times, closing windows and logging out of a program before pushing his chair back and standing up. "It's probably nothing," he added to remind himself and her. "Every once in a while a camera just goes out."

"I thought you said this was the best security system on the market."

"I said Messina Diamonds has the best security system on the market. Not all our clients can afford the best. The eleventh floor is Lee, Oban and Associates, a law firm. Their system is merely very good. But even the best system can suffer from a technical glitch. It's why we have redundant systems."

All of which was true. Any other night and he

wouldn't even bother to check on it. Of course, any other night and he wouldn't even be here to check on it.

"So what do we do?" she asked, following him down the hall to the elevators. "You're not going to call the police, are you?"

"To check out a downed camera? No." He shot her a droll look. "We'll go down to the security offices on the second floor to reboot the camera. Then we'll go up to the eleventh floor to double-check that everything's fine."

"Maybe this is a stupid question, but shouldn't there be a guard or someone on duty down there?" She looked pointedly at his phone. "Or was that the call you just made?"

"He's probably just out on his rounds." No point in telling her that even if the guard was on his rounds, he should have answered his phone.

As they waited for the elevator, he prayed that chattiness of hers would vanish. Naturally, it didn't. This just wasn't his night.

"If the building's security offices are on the second floor, why do you need three whole floors up here?"

"These are the business offices."

"When you say the business offices you mean…" She left the question dangling.

"The whole international operation is run from the business office," he explained.

"The whole international operation, huh? I see." She

paused before asking, in an overly casual tone, "How big is McCain Security, exactly?"

"We have offices in L.A., New York, Chicago, San Francisco and San Jose. As well as smaller offices in Toronto, London, Paris, Antwerp and Tokyo."

"Oh."

He slanted her a look and she seemed to be purposefully keeping her expression very blank. "How big did you think it was?"

"Oh. That big. About." The elevator doors opened on the second floor and she followed him out. "Sure, that's what I was thinking."

"You thought it was just Messina Diamonds, didn't you?"

For a long time, when he'd first gotten out of the army, it had been just Messina Diamonds. Of course, the mining company had been fledgling back then, with barely enough investment capital for operating expenses. Randolph Messina, Derek's father, had paid Quinn in company stock. By the time Messina Diamonds had gone public a few years ago, McCain Security was a leader in the security industry.

"Well," she said sheepishly. "It's not like I've been glued to your career."

"On Wednesday you said you knew what I did for a living. I assumed you'd done your research."

"I read the papers. It's hard to avoid all the references to McCain Security in the business section." A blush crept into her cheeks. "But generally I try not to pay attention." Then, as if she'd revealed more than she intended, she added in an overly cheerful voice, "So all the times we used to talk about traveling the world and waking up in a different country every week. And now it turns out you actually do that."

They approached the doors and he mindlessly did the security protocols and led her through the utilitarian reception area to another set of locked doors.

"It gets old after a while," he admitted. Then when he realized that sounded pathetic, he added, "What about you? You always wanted to see the world. Do you travel much?"

"Oh, sure." Her tone was a little too bright. "A couple of years ago a girlfriend and I went to Cancun for the weekend."

"Sounds nice."

"It was great!" she said with far more enthusiasm than a weekend in Mexico usually garnered. "We stayed at a very nice Holiday Inn."

He should have been gloating. Yet somehow it made him a little sad that her dreams hadn't panned out. His next words were out of his mouth before he thought better of it. "I guess you regret it now."

"Regret what?"

He concentrated on unlocking the final door. "Not having more faith in me."

She placed her hand on his arm. "I always had faith in you."

He shook her hand off as he led her through the door into a room dominated by a bank of computers and monitors. He yanked back the rolling chair and sat in front of one of the computers.

"You believe me, don't you?"

He ignored her question as he opened up a program, feigning far more concentration than the act required. After few minutes, he rocked back in the chair. "This'll take a few minutes and then we'll go up to the eleventh floor."

"You never answered my question."

He shrugged. "What does it matter?"

"It matters to me." She pulled a chair close to his and sat. He still faced the bank of computer monitors, so she was talking to his profile. "I always knew you would do amazing things. I never doubted that for a minute."

Just let it go, he told himself. *This isn't worth it.*

But he didn't let it go. "Which explains perfectly why you filed for an annulment before the ink was dry on our marriage certificate."

"Is that what you thought all these years? That I ended our marriage because I didn't believe in you?"

But he still didn't meet her gaze. There were some conversations that just weren't worth having. That was a lesson he'd learned a long time ago. It was a tactic that had served him well growing up and in his time in the army. Keep quiet. Keep your head down. Avoid the tough conversation. Focus on the task at hand.

So instead of responding to Evie, he stared dead ahead at the monitor as if the series of blinking lights and the words "Camera 1121 Offline" were the key to all of life's mysteries.

"I guess that is what you thought." Since he wasn't talking to her, she kept talking to herself, filling in his part of the conversation with an exaggeratedly pessimistic view. "You must have thought I was just some fickle rich girl. Only interested in a good time, until—"

"It wasn't your fault," he said, even though he knew he should have kept his mouth shut.

"What?" She seemed so surprised by his interruption, she merely gaped at him.

"I said, it wasn't your fault." God, did he really want to hash through this? No. Not. Even. A little. "Of course you were spoiled. It was just how you were raised. You'd gotten everything you ever wanted. It was second nature for you to rebel against your father. I should have realized our relationship—"

"Oh my gosh." She shot to her feet, knocking her chair back. "You actually believe that."

He spun his own chair out to face her, surprised at her vehement reaction.

"I can't believe that you actually thought that about me." Shock quickly gave way to anger and she swatted at his shoulders with her tiny beaded clutch. "That I was just some spoiled. Fickle." She punctuated each adjective with a thump. "Rebellious. Rich—"

He grabbed her wrist before she could land another blow. How dare she act offended? "That actually hurts, you know."

Since he was still sitting, she had to lean down to get in his face. She glared into his upturned eyes. "It's supposed to hurt. How do you think it feels to find out that the man you once loved has dismissed you as having every quality you most despise?"

What the hell was wrong with her? He was the wounded party here. "If you didn't want me to think you're fickle, then you shouldn't have filed for annulment within twenty-four hours of promising to love me forever."

"You were in jail. What was I supposed to do?"

His gut clenched with anger. "You could have had a little faith." He purposely threw her word back at her. "I wasn't going to be in jail forever. You could have waited. But I guess your vision for your future didn't involve a husband who'd been in jail."

"And that's really what you thought of me?" Some of her anger was sputtering out, giving way to a tone full of confusion. "That I filed for annulment merely because you'd become—" she floundered for a word "—I don't know, inconvenient? Because you didn't fit into my plan?"

"What was I supposed to think? The next day your father showed up. He explained that he'd given you an ultimatum. If we stayed married, he was cutting you off." Cyrus Montgomery had stood outside Quinn's jail cell for more than an hour "explaining things" to him. Cowboy boots planted wide, he'd rocked back and forth, working the rim of his hat with his hands as he told Quinn about the kind of things a girl like his Genevieve needed to be happy. Things Quinn hadn't believed Evie needed. So he'd waited for her to show up and throw her father's words back in his face. And she never had.

"I didn't think it would matter to you," he admitted

now about those hours he'd spent in the county jail. "But then four hours later, your lawyer showed up with annulment papers."

"You could have had a little faith." She deliberately repeated his words back to him. "I signed those papers because I had to."

"Because your father was going to cut you off if you didn't," he countered.

"I didn't care about my father's money." Her eyes were wide and imploring, covered with a sheen of tears. "I've never cared about it. That wasn't the deal my father made me. If I got an annulment, he'd drop the charges against you. I signed those papers because if I didn't, my father was going to have you indicted. The charges against you were very serious. You would have gone to prison."

He was silent for a long time, absorbing her words like a shock wave as his own anguish tore through him. Finally, quietly, he said, "You should have told me."

She straightened. "I didn't want to risk you not signing the papers. I was protecting you the only way I knew how. If it hadn't been for me, you never would have been in that mess."

He stood and tipped her chin up so she was looking up at him. His heart felt as if it was being crushed in a vice. He spoke slowly but gently. "Those charges your father brought against me never would have stuck."

Tears spilled onto her ivory cheeks. Her anguish seemed to match his own. "Maybe they wouldn't have. But what if they had?" Her voice broke on the question and she cleared her throat before continuing. "I couldn't live with that. Besides, I didn't think it was the end of our relationship. I never dreamed that you were going to be so pigheaded and leave town right after signing the papers." Her voice grew thin. "I thought you'd come back to me."

"Your father told me you didn't want anything to do with me. That you never wanted to see me again."

"I waited for weeks—" Her voice broke.

The image of her waiting for him lodged in his mind. He'd been in her childhood bedroom only once. It had been a delicate pink concoction of frothy netting and ruffled canopies. He pictured her now, sitting on that bed, knees curled to her chest, inky dyed hair hanging in her eyes, just waiting for him.

Evie, who always tried to be so tough, but who was more frail than she wanted to admit beneath all that brass and bravado. Evie, who'd been crushed by her mother's death, who'd fought so desperately for the tiniest shreds of attention from her father.

God. The idea of her waiting and waiting for him to return. And him never coming back for her.

Thinking about it now, he felt as if he couldn't breathe. As if his chest was going to be crushed by the weight of his emotions.

And there she was now, flashing him a game little smile, despite the tears streaking her face and the slight tremble of her hand as she brushed back a wayward lock of hair. She was trying her damnedest to pretend his desertion hadn't crushed her very soul. But he knew it had.

At the time, he'd thought the worst of her and still it had killed him to leave her. He couldn't imagine how much more it must have hurt her.

"Then I guess we're both stupid for believing my father's lies," she said with a shrug.

Stupid? Stupid didn't begin to describe how he felt now.

"For my part," she continued, "I assumed when you got out of jail, you'd come find me. When you didn't, I thought—"

He didn't let her finish. He pulled her into his arms and kissed her. Pouring into that single kiss all the apology and regret he'd never be able to voice. He'd never be able to make up for the pain he'd caused her. For the years they'd lost. Words alone would never be enough to express his remorse. He could only keep kissing her and pray that that would be enough.

He could have gone on kissing her forever. He was about to tell her exactly that when the flashing light on the monitor caught his eye. The feed to the camera was live again and the picture on the screen was not what he expected.

The monitor displayed a wide-angle shot of the warren of cubicles in the lawyer's office on the eleventh floor. He was almost too distracted to notice. But something on the edge of the image frame caught his attention.

Leaving Evie where she stood, he dropped into the chair and pulled up an enlarged image of the live feed. And there, almost out of camera range, he saw it. One of the acoustic tiles in the ceiling sat lopsided. As if someone had moved it aside and then put it back without checking to make sure it sat correctly.

Quinn whipped out his cell phone and used the page feature to get J.D. on the line. "We've got a situation on eleven. I want you to go to the safe and check on the diamonds."

J.D. responded instantly, saying he'd report back as soon as he'd done it, but Quinn barely registered his words, trusting the other man to handle it. Instead he was painfully aware of Evie as she rested a hand on his shoulder and leaned over to gaze at the image on the computer screen.

She pointed a finger to the ceiling tile. "That's it, isn't it?"

"Maybe." He zoomed in further on the picture, trying to force his mind into action, looking for other inconsistencies. "Or maybe it's nothing. It's a pretty laid-back office for a group of lawyers. They're always hanging college flags and crap from the acoustic supports. They were probably just careless."

"But you don't think so," she guessed. "Or you wouldn't have contacted J.D." When he didn't confirm her theory, she asked, "But would anyone break into a lawyer's office?"

He knew the way her mind worked and could tell from the look in her eyes that scenes from John Grisham novels were flashing through her mind, with laundered money, mob connections and confidential papers being shredded in the dead of night. Before her imagination could spin too far out of control, Quinn spoke.

"They wouldn't. But the eleventh floor is the floor directly below the first floor of McCain Security."

It took her a minute to realize the significance. When she did, he felt the muscles of her hand tighten on his shoulder. "Which means," she said aloud, "that it's the floor closest to the diamonds that's not actually part of either McCain or Messina."

"Exactly. With the right set of tools and some fancy climbing, someone small could access the crawl space and from there, the duct work. It's a long climb up to the twenty-first floor, but not impossible."

As they made their way back to the elevators, he wanted to offer her some reassurances. But what could he say, really? There was a good chance she'd been right. Her brother may even now be trying to steal more than ten million dollars worth of diamonds. And if Corbin was, then it was Quinn's job to stop him.

"I thought you said there weren't any diamonds here tonight."

"I lied."

Quinn's phone rang as if to echo the grim fatality of his words. When he answered it, Evie heard a string of cursing from the other end. J.D. had just checked. The diamonds were gone.

A wave of nausea washed over her as blood rushed from her head. Mindlessly, she groped for a chair. Something to hold on to. Anything to ground herself.

Then she felt Quinn's steady arm under her hand. His voice was a low tremor registering beneath the ringing in her ears. He guided her to a chair as he finished the conversation with J.D. in a few curt words.

She squeezed her eyes shut to clear her mind. Of course he had lied about there not being any diamonds here. That's what her gut had told her earlier. She'd just hoped she was wrong. Now, she tried to narrow her attention past her shock and confusion to focus on Quinn's gaze.

"Are you okay?" he asked.

"I'm fine." She shook off his touch, even though it seemed the only thing anchoring her down.

"You looked like you were about to faint there for a minute."

She stifled a derogatory snort. "I don't faint." She felt a ridiculous surge of resentment. "Why aren't you upset? You should be at least as freaked out about this as I am."

But as soon as she said it, she realized he was just as agitated. He just kept it buried deeply inside. His eyes had narrowed to grim slits, and he'd clenched his jaw so tightly it looked as if it were chiseled from granite. This stony silence of his spoke more than her near fainting.

"I'm sorry," she muttered, forcing herself to her feet. "You probably want to go back to Messina Diamonds."

The absurdity of that statement gurgled up inside her, threatening to escape as hysterical laughter. She was sorry for *delaying* him? If she was going to be sorry, there were a whole lot of other things to be sorry for.

Still, he nodded tightly and placed a hand at her

back, guiding her toward the elevator. As the door began to close behind them, he said, "Evie, about your brother…"

"I know. If he's involved you're going to have to do everything in your power to find him and have him arrested."

"*If* he's involved?"

"Yes," she said. "*If* he's involved."

"Evie, you can't afford to be naive. Not after all of this. Your brother is definitely involved."

"No. We don't know that. Not yet, anyway. All we have so far is conjecture."

"Hey, you're the one who came to me," Quinn pointed out.

"Yes. Exactly." She turned to glare at him, crossing her arms over her chest against a sudden chill. "I came to you because I thought you could help. And you swore to me that the system was unbreakable. That Messina Diamonds had a top-of-the-line system. Corbin wouldn't be able to steal a pen from the receptionist's desk. Isn't that what you said to me?"

He didn't answer, but his gaze narrowed even further. She sucked in a deep breath as she forced herself to focus. Quinn wasn't the enemy here. This blow had to be hitting him just as hard. After all, the system he'd staked his honor on had failed. His company's biggest client had just been robbed. Right out from under his nose.

"I did say that. There must have been someone on the inside," Quinn said slowly. As if he were just now figuring through it. "He couldn't have gotten past that system. Someone had to have shut it off for him."

"Who?"

"I don't know. Until I do, everyone is a suspect."

"Well, that's not how I see it. Until you can prove otherwise to me, I'm going to assume my brother is innocent."

"Don't be an idiot."

"Corbin is the only family I have." She rounded on Quinn. "And I'm the only family he has. I'm not just going to desert him when he needs me most. I'm not going to abandon him like—"

Like you abandoned me.

But she sucked the words back into her mouth without saying them. Some things should never be said aloud. They hurt too much. Revealed too much.

She shifted to face the elevator doors again. "Everyone needs to have someone who believes in them wholeheartedly. Someone who loves them no matter what. For Corbin I'm that person."

"You're the one who suspected him in the first place," he reminded her again. "Just a few minutes ago you believed him capable of this."

"I believed he could be manipulated into helping." She could see from the glint of cynicism in Quinn's gaze that he didn't see the difference. How could she explain to him what she barely understood herself? "Of course I believe it's possible he's involved. But still he's my brother. I have to have faith in him. I have to believe he didn't do this of his own accord. Until you can bring me proof, hard evidence…"

She never learned what Quinn's reaction might have been to her seemingly blind faith in Corbin. The elevator doors whooshed open, thrusting the two of them out of the quiet into the noisy bustle of a gala in progress. None of the guests knew what had happened yet. She barely knew herself.

Six

Things happened quickly after that. The police arrived. And then the FBI. Everyone in the building was detained.

All things considered, the guests took it surprisingly well. The caterers brought out more food. The band continued to play. The party atmosphere remained. People seemed thrilled to be on-site for the most glamorous of all possible crimes: a diamond heist.

Perhaps it was understandable. A robbery this bold and daring that had taken place just a few floors away from a party with hundreds of guests—it was the stuff of legends. It would be big news in Dallas. Probably all over the States. The guests here tonight would dine out on this story for years.

Evie, however, didn't feel quite so titillated. After all,

somehow, her stupid, gullible brother had been roped in to this mess. Of all the idiotic stunts he'd been involved with, this really took the cake. And to think, he was supposed to be the smart one in the family. Well, apparently a genius IQ only got you so far.

Feeling tense and slightly nauseated, she scanned the room looking for Quinn. Police detectives were milling through the crowd, sorting people into groups. Everyone would have to be searched before they were allowed to leave. Information would be taken and IDs would be checked. Derek and J.D., along with the FBI agents, had disappeared into one of the offices upstairs. Quinn had gone with them, but Evie thought she'd seen him return a few minutes ago.

She'd heard a rumor filtering through the crowd that the FBI was questioning J.D. and Quinn. If the system was truly unbreakable, then McCain Security itself was suspect. Which did wonders for her nausea.

Suddenly, despite her big noble speech about trusting her brother, she felt a surge of doubt. What if her brother *was* guilty?

No. She couldn't think about that. Couldn't consider that possibility.

Yes, she respected Quinn. Sure, she desired him. She even felt bad—okay, really bad—about how things had ended fourteen years ago. But her loyalty belonged to her brother. He was her family. Corbin may be a screwup, but he'd always loved her. Always been there for her. She couldn't let her doubts get the better of her. Not yet.

While she searched the crowd for Quinn, she contemplated what had happened back there in the security office, before all this garbage with her brother hit the proverbial fan. Quinn had kissed her. Really kissed her. Like, I-want-to-go-on-kissing-you-forever kissed her.

She moved through the crowded room, looking for a place to sit for a minute alone, some respite from the buzzing chatter of the guests. She followed one of the waiters through a door at the back of the room that led to a service hall.

She was only a few steps through the swinging door when she heard a voice behind her. "Hold up there, miss." Turning, she found one of the suited FBI agents holding up his badge. "Agent Ryan. You're not allowed to leave yet."

The FBI agent towered over her. He had the build and demeanor of a defensive linebacker. Staring up into his humorless face, she felt her throat close off. His very presence was a reminder that she should not be thinking about Quinn at all. She had enough on her emotional plate right now just worrying about her brother.

"I wasn't planning on leaving," she explained. "I just wanted to get away from the crowd."

"You're the suspect's sister, correct?"

A wave of guilt swamped her. Somehow, facing this FBI agent made everything more real. Dear lord, please let Corbin not be involved in this. Please, please let him be innocent.

"One of them. I mean, my brother is one of the suspects. I'm sure he's not the only one. Surely there are several…" The more she rambled, the narrower Agent Ryan's gaze got. She swallowed. "Yes. Corbin Montgomery is my brother."

"I'll need to question you before you leave."

"Certainly." That should be easy enough. She knew very little and had nothing to hide.

A moment later, Quinn appeared in the hall behind the FBI agent. Quinn spoke quietly with the man for a moment, then the agent nodded his understanding and ducked back into the room.

She took it as a good sign that Agent Ryan seemed confident trusting her with Quinn. Surely if Quinn was a suspect the agent wouldn't be leaving them alone together.

"Ah, my savior," she said lamely. As serious as always, Quinn didn't bother to pretend to laugh, which, under the circumstances, she actually appreciated. "I wasn't trying to leave. I just needed a moment away from the crowd."

He nodded his understanding. "I can wait with you."

His words sent a shiver of dread down her spine. "I guess then I really am at the top of the most-wanted list for this one, then?"

"As long as you don't hide anything, you won't be a suspect. But you're definitely someone the agents want to talk to."

She wrapped her arms around her body and rubbed at the chilled skin of her biceps. Why did they always keep office buildings so cold? "You're trying to be diplomatic. How reassuring," she muttered. Sarcastically.

"It's probably not as bad as all that." Quinn tugged off his jacket and draped it over her shoulders. Turning her toward the catering station at the end of the hall, he guided her in that direction. "Come on. Let's see if we can get you something warm to drink. Maybe they have some cocoa or something."

"You're offering me cocoa?" she asked in disbelief. "Things must be worse than I thought." He'd given her hell about everything from her morals to her housing and now didn't know what to say to her? "I already know you lied to me earlier about there not being any diamonds here. Can you at least tell me how much is missing?"

"Last week there was what looked like a simple clerical error. A shipment of diamonds that should have gone to the New York office was shipped here instead." His shoulders were taut with tension, his movements as terse as his tone.

Her stomach clenched and she had to swallow down bile before she could ask, "How much were they worth?"

"The mistake wasn't caught until this afternoon when they were unloaded. It appeared someone had simply typed in the wrong code on a packing invoice. It seemed innocent enough. The guy didn't even realize he'd done it. When the mistake was caught, Derek arranged for them to be stored here overnight and shipped out in the morning. They were going to be in the office less than twelve hours."

"How much were they worth?" Every minute he didn't answer, her anxiety increased. If he didn't want to tell her, it must be bad. Beyond bad.

"It's hard to say for sure. Probably close to ten million dollars."

She felt the blood drain from her head, leaving her woozy and weak. "So much?"

"On the black market, they'll probably sell for a bit less. These days anything that comes out of a cutting house in Antwerp is laser cut with the Messina Diamonds logo and a serial number, which means in order to be sold again, they have to be recut. But once that's done—"

"They'll be untraceable." She finished the sentence for him. "That's a huge amount of money. But I don't understand. How could anyone have possibly known the diamonds would be here tonight? Didn't you say there are rarely diamonds here at all?"

"That's the point. They couldn't have known. They must have had an inside man."

Both Evie and Quinn sat in silence as he drove her home. Naturally, she'd protested that she didn't need the ride. He'd expected that and eventually his insistence had worn her down. Under other circumstances, he might have felt guilty for taking advantage of her emotional exhaustion.

Tonight, with ten million dollars worth of diamonds stolen out from under his nose, he didn't have time for guilt.

As he steered his car off Highway 35E and onto Illinois Avenue, he glanced over and noticed Evie staring at him.

When he met her gaze, she said, "You didn't have to drive me home, you know."

"So you keep saying. But it's late." A valid argument since by the time the FBI agents had started letting people leave, it was after two in the morning.

"And you probably worry about my neighborhood being unsafe, but you can rest assured that I'm always there at two in the morning and nothing bad has happened to me yet."

"It's no trouble," he said simply.

She sighed, a sound filled with more exasperation than resignation. "It'll be trouble for me in the morning when I have to call a cab to drive me downtown to pick up my car."

"I'll drive you."

"Which brings me back to my point. Your biggest client was just robbed. Surely you have better things to do than chauffeur me around Dallas."

"Now that the robbery is over, it's in the hands of the FBI. There's not much for me to do."

Evie harrumphed. "You don't seriously expect me to believe that, do you? That you're just going to step aside and let the FBI find out who's behind this?"

She always had been smart. It wouldn't take her long to figure out the real reason he was sticking so close to her side. He wasn't going to break down and tell her first. If he was lucky, she was too tired to figure it out tonight.

When he didn't say anything, she kept talking. "No. I know you. You're going to be out there, tracking down leads or whatever it is you security types do in this situation. You'll be interviewing witnesses or tailing suspects or something."

"J.D. can handle most of that. He's fairly trustworthy."

"*Fairly* trustworthy? I thought he was your second in command?"

"He is."

"Boy." She shook her head. "When you said everybody was a suspect you really meant it. You don't trust anyone, do you?"

"It's my job to be suspicious of everyone. I learned long ago that most people will disappoint you."

She was silent for a long moment, looking out the window with her head resting back. Her posture was either one of relaxation or pensive contemplation. He hoped she'd fallen asleep, but doubted it.

Without moving, she murmured, "I'm sorry."

"You're not responsible for your brother's actions."

"That's not what I'm apologizing for." She looked over at him. "I'm sorry that what happened between us twisted you into this bitter, distrusting man."

There was that pity again. Damn it.

His hands clenched the steering wheel. "Is that really how you see me?"

He glanced in her direction. In the flickering light of the passing streetlights, he saw a frown crease her forehead.

"How am I supposed to answer that? On the surface you're very successful. You've made all of this money. But you have no one you can really trust. Not even your second in command. You seem to have lost all faith in humanity."

Forcing a smile, he quipped, "I'm the son of an alcoholic. I never had much faith in humanity to begin with."

"No." She shook her head. "You weren't like this when we were younger. Despite how you were raised, you had so much hope. And you trusted me completely. Now…"

She trailed off and abruptly she stiffened. "Wait a second. You *don't* trust me. You think I could be involved. You're…" she sputtered, waving her hands around for effect. "You're tailing a suspect. You're following me!"

He braced himself to get whacked by her purse again. "Not you," he began to protest, but she didn't let him finish.

"Yes, me. You're in the car with me, aren't you?"

In the flicker of the passing streetlights, he'd have sworn he could see her glaring maliciously at him.

She harrumphed again, turning in her seat, staring straight ahead with her arms crossed over her chest. "I can't believe you think I had something to do with this."

"Not you," he repeated as he turned off Illinois into her neighborhood. "Corbin."

But apparently she was too far into her rant to listen to him. "If I'd had anything to do with this at all, why would I have stuck around tonight as long as I did? Huh? Wouldn't I have just skedaddled out of there as soon as you turned your back on me?"

He pulled the car to a stop in front of her house and flicked the ignition off. "Let's go inside and talk about this there."

"Well," she said, hopping out of the car. "I don't suppose I have much of a choice, do I? Since you're going to tail me anyway."

So much for her being emotionally exhausted. He climbed out of the hybrid Lexus and beeped it locked, watching her flounce up the flower-rimmed walkway to her front door.

The Tudor-style cottage with its gentle sloping roof and alcoved front door was surprisingly welcoming. In the dark, the disrepair of the neighboring turn-of-the-century houses was less noticeable. The lantern that hung over the front door cast a golden circle of light over Evie, bringing out the fiery tones in her hair. When he came up behind her, she glared at him over her shoulder as she rammed her key into the lock.

"Don't think I'm going to offer you a drink."

"I wouldn't presume."

She marched straight through the living room to a bedroom just off the dining room. Since she was furious with him, there was no point in not following.

Yep, she was well and truly pissed off. And he couldn't say that he blamed her. In the past few days he'd insulted her, propositioned her and dismissed her fears—which turned out to be well-grounded. Now she thought he was accusing her of being involved in grand larceny. He'd be pissed at him, too.

Add to that the fact that he'd kissed her senseless in the security room and they still hadn't talked about that… Well, he was lucky she hadn't started swatting him with that lethal purse of hers again.

He followed her into the bedroom. She'd already pulled off the gown and it lay haphazardly over the jewel-toned quilt. On the far side of the room, she'd left the door just ajar and light slashed through the opening. From the other side he heard water running.

"Look, I know you're angry right now—" he began.

"Oh, do you?" The water cut off and a second later, the bathroom door swung open.

Evie stood before him, wrapped in a hot-pink silky robe, her hair loose about her shoulders, her face devoid of makeup. She held a towel in her hands. Her cheeks were flushed, either with her heightened emotions or from being scrubbed clean. The sight of her there, haloed by the light spilling into the room from the bathroom, nearly took his breath away so that he forgot what he'd been about to say.

She apparently wasn't similarly struck because she paused in front of him only for a second, before pushing past him.

"Maybe you've just spent too much of your life thinking badly of me. But I would never be involved in something like this."

Instead of waiting for his answer, she strode to her dresser and began pulling off her jewelry. He crossed to stand behind her, stilling her hand at her ear.

"I don't think you're involved." He met her gaze in the reflection of the mirror and held it. "I never thought that. But right now, you're still the best lead I have."

She frowned, turning to face him. "But—"

"Even you can't deny your brother's involved some-how. The police will be looking for him. Probably watching his house. But you're right. I can't just stand by and do nothing."

"So you decided to stay with me." She finished the thought for him, her tone sapped of its earlier anger. Her forehead was creased with a frown and she held one hand at her ear, absently toying with the earring that dangled there. "Then why didn't you say that earlier? Why let me get all worked up over nothing and yell and scream at you?"

"You've had a rough night," he explained. "You have every right to be angry."

"At my brother. He's the one who got me into this mess. Not you."

"But your brother isn't here. And you needed to yell at someone."

"Oh." Her voice came out hushed and reverent. "That's very sweet."

"No." He said it through almost gritted teeth. "It isn't."

"You were always very chivalrous. Even when we were kids." With languid slowness, she removed her other earring and set it on the dresser. "I never understood how you stayed so gentle and kind despite how you were raised."

"I wasn't gentle and kind."

The words made him sound weak. Vulnerable.

He hadn't been. He'd just known when to walk away from a fight. How to escape notice.

His father had been a sloppy drunk but not a violent one. Quinn had been nine the one and only time Child Protective Services had removed him from his father's care. Two weeks with foster parents had convinced him home wasn't as bad as the alternative. Besides, his father needed him. So he'd become an expert at caring for himself, at not attracting attention.

How he'd ever attracted hers, he'd never know.

Now, she was watching him with her head tilted slightly to the side. "Do you remember when we first started dating?"

Of course he did. He'd been working at Mann's Auto and she'd come in to have her oil changed. She'd spent the whole time on the cell phone arguing with her father about something. When he came to the waiting room to tell her that her car was ready, she'd looked him up and down before saying, *"You're that kid from my algebra class. You wanna take me out Friday night?"*

"It was weeks before you even kissed me," she said now. Then she chuckled. "I think that's why I kept dating you. If we'd fooled around that first night, I probably never would have gone on a second date."

That first date had been etched in his memory. He'd known at the time that she was just using him to get back at her father. That hadn't taken a genius to figure out. To be honest, he hadn't even minded. She'd been so damn beautiful.

"No," she continued now. "At the end of the night, I kept waiting for you to make your move. But you didn't even touch me."

"I wanted to," he admitted now. As they'd sat in her car under a streetlight, her skin had looked impossibly soft. Almost luminescent. Just like it did now. He'd known that dating him ranked somewhere between dying her hair black, which she done on and off throughout high school, and getting a tattoo, which—as far as he knew—she'd never actually done, despite her numerous threats. He'd known he was little more than a rebellion, yet he hadn't cared.

She'd been too pretty and he'd felt too fortunate to be in her company for her motives to matter to him. Even then, she'd had this amazing mixture of vibrancy and frailty. With her curly auburn hair and her pale-as-moonlight skin, she looked like one of the women in the Pre-Raphaelite posters their English teacher had plastered all over the walls.

He'd sat there beside her in the car knowing she was waiting for him to kiss her. Randy teenage boy that he'd been, there'd been a hundred—no, probably a thousand—things he wanted to do to her. And she was just rebellious enough to let him. But then he'd looked down at his hands with their rough palms and grease-rimmed nails.

"My hands were dirty," he said now. Why he admitted it, he wasn't sure. Maybe it was because of all the things he wanted to tell her but couldn't, because—Christ—what was he supposed to say? *I'm really sorry I broke your heart fourteen years ago and let me make it up to you by sending your brother to prison.*

Yeah. That was probably the big romantic gesture she'd been dreaming of since she was a girl.

No, he couldn't be with her until this business with her brother was settled. Until he knew how things stood, he wasn't going to make any promises he couldn't keep.

So instead of saying all the things he couldn't tell her, he talked about the one thing he could: how he used to feel about her, back when their lives had been less complicated. Not that things had ever been uncomplicated between them.

She gave him a funny look, head quirked. "Your hands?" she prodded.

"When you work in a body shop, your hands never really get clean."

But man, he'd wanted to kiss her. He'd wanted it more than he'd ever wanted anything else. More than he'd wanted to drive the 1966 Mustang he'd been rebuilding for Mr. Kopfler. More than he'd wanted to leave Mason and never return. That's how much he'd wanted it. "I was afraid I'd leave grease marks on your clothes."

So he hadn't touched her. They had been on more than a dozen dates before he'd worked up the courage to run his dirty, solder-roughened fingertips across her cheek.

Maybe that's why it had been so easy for her father to convince him Evie didn't love him. Quinn hadn't ever really believed she did.

She moved toward him slowly, her sensual hips swaying beneath the robe. "Your hands aren't dirty now."

Her words surprised him, snapped him out of his memories and back into the moment. He looked down at his hands, half expecting to see those long-ago smears of grease.

Her lips gave a twitch of either amusement or nervousness. "You were looking like maybe you wanted—"

He didn't let her finish the sentence. Sometimes she talked too damn much anyway. Instead, he pulled her close and covered her mouth with his. Her mouth was warm beneath his. Her lips pliant and moist. Soft. Welcoming.

Unlike the previous night, there was no anger in this kiss. No rebellion. No resistance. Only a gentle acceptance. Unlike earlier tonight, there was no grief. No remorse. No penitence. Only stirrings of desire. Of hope.

He brushed his fingertips across her cheek. Her skin was as velvety as he remembered. Pure heaven. He could spend decades exploring her skin. Aeons memorizing the texture. He heard her groan low in her throat, and an answering moan rose up in his chest.

She bucked against him, one bare foot coming off the ground to rub along the back of his calf. Taking the cue from her, he sank his hands into her buttocks. He lifted her against him, grinding his erection against the vee between her legs. She parted her thighs and he automatically stepped between them, walking her backward until her weight rested on the edge of her dresser. Her robe had fallen open so that the only thing separating their bodies were his pants and a delicate wisp of silken fabric. He was one step away from heaven.

His hands slipped inside her robe to bare flesh at her waist. He explored her skin with a hungry neediness, relishing the quiver of her stomach muscles, the rapid rise and fall of her chest, the heavy weight of her breast in his hand. There must have been a thousand metaphors for how desperately he wanted her. Metaphors about starving men and feasts, desert treks and oases. None of them conveyed the depth of his desire.

He didn't want to merely have sex with her. He wanted to consume her. To wrap his entire body around her and absorb her through his skin. To possess her so completely she wouldn't know where he ended and she began. So completely she'd never again doubt how he felt.

Her hands seemed everywhere at once. Burrowing through his hair. Tugging at his buttons. Unfastening his belt. Her skin was hot against his. As enflamed as he felt. He slipped his finger under the silken fabric of her panties and found the moist center of her. When he ran the pad of his thumb across the nub of her desire, she ripped her mouth from his, tipped her head back and groaned. The guttural sound came from low in the throat and his body leapt in response.

He simply couldn't get enough of her. He might have taken her right there on the dresser, if he hadn't felt a persistent buzzing from his pocket. His cell phone. He tried to ignore it. It rang. Then the pager function bleeped. Then the text message alert chimed. When the whole sequence started again, he broke free from the kiss and, panting, rested his forehead against hers. Willing his body back under his control. Suddenly, he felt seventeen again. Desperate. Needy. Unworthy.

He pulled his phone from his pocket. Instead of obliterating it, the way he wanted to, he pulled up the text message. It read: *Check in. News about CM. J.D.*

* * *

Quinn had pulled away from her so quickly, it left her head spinning. One minute he was kissing her, the next he was tugging her robe closed and stepping away from her. He left her sitting on her dresser. Panting, wanting, *needing*.

He stood with his back to her for a moment, his posture tense. When he turned back, he was buttoning his jacket. He shoved a hand through his hair as if to smooth it down, but it did more damage than good.

"What the—" she began.

"This isn't the time." His voice was rough with unspoken desire. Desire he could have sated just now, but chose not to. Why?

Before she could ask, he was heading for the door. Running, practically. She caught up with him at the front door.

"Where are you going? I thought I was your best lead. That you were going to stick by my side until Corbin contacted me."

His eyes searched her face and for an instant she thought he would cave, but then he said, "I'll watch the house from the car. I trust you'll let me know if he calls."

"Wait a second. After all your talk about how dangerous my neighborhood is, you're going to spend the night in your car? That's crazy."

His lips twitched ever so slightly in amusement. "I guess you've convinced me it's safe after all."

Or you think it's more dangerous in here.

She bit back the words as she watched him walk out her door.

Once again Quinn had left her unsatisfied. Was this just more of his twisted revenge? Or was Quinn simply too honorable to take advantage of her?

Neither answer was good for her psyche. If she was honest with herself, she felt a bit as if she were back in high school, twisted into knots all over again. She wished she could pretend that what she felt now was an illusion. A mere echo of her feelings then. But she was very much afraid that things had progressed beyond that.

The boy Quinn had been had spoken to her teenage self in a way no one else had. His quiet seriousness, his respectful—almost worshipful—attention, his deeply engrained sense of honor. They had all been a balm to the restlessness of her soul. This new, adult Quinn had so many of those same qualities, but there was something else, too. His commanding presence. His strength. And still, the sense of honor, which he had somehow maintained despite his cynicism. He may be distrustful, but he wasn't cold. He wasn't unfeeling. In fact, it seemed almost as if he felt things more deeply.

And none of this was good for her. She didn't want to fall for Quinn all over again. Not when so much stood between them.

After all, between protecting her brother and protecting Quinn, how could she possibly protect her own heart?

Seven

"Tell me she's not involved."

Quinn regretted the words—the sheer vulnerability of them—the moment they left his mouth. However, his regret didn't keep him from holding his breath while he waited for a response. Besides, he'd had hours to think of a better question, but that was the only one to come to mind.

He'd been on the phone with J.D. on and off throughout the night. Until now, he'd let J.D. do most of the talking. The news had ranged from pinning down where the security system had been overridden to picking up an accomplice in the airport. None of the news had been good. At least not in terms of exonerating Corbin.

J.D., who'd just climbed into the passenger seat of

Quinn's Lexus, tugged on the zipper of his coat and ignored his boss's statement. "It's freezing in here. You sat in here all night?"

"Freezing" was an exaggeration, as was "all night," since it was hovering near fifty and he'd only been here about three hours, it being just after six now. He'd barely noticed the cold. He'd spent every second of those three-plus hours thinking about Evie. Reliving the past, replaying the kiss, wondering what the hell he should have done differently last night. Frankly, it hadn't occurred to him to feel cold.

"What have you found out?" Quinn asked J.D.

"Not much." J.D. handed over a folder, then cupped his hands and puffed into them. "You want to turn on the heat in here?"

"Wimp," Quinn muttered as he flipped open the folder and scanned the first few pages.

Beside him, J.D. shifted in his seat, tucking his hands inside his coat pockets. "Hey, what can I say?" J.D snapped his omnipresent gum. "I'm a sand and surf kind of guy."

Quinn ignored his second in command as he continued reading. His feeling of dread grew stronger. The situation was about what he'd expected. Damn it. Sometimes he hated being right. Evie had wanted proof. Well, here it was. He didn't know if he'd have the heart to tell her.

He snapped the folder closed. "Got anything else for me?"

"Coffee?"

It took a second for J.D.'s offer to register through Quinn's preoccupation. Finally, he smiled and nodded. "Sure. You have a doughnut to go with it?"

"I'll check." J.D. made a call on his cell phone. Before he was even finished talking, someone hopped out of the car behind them, which J.D. had driven up in only moments before. The woman—Alyssa—from J.D.'s team approached Quinn's car, tapped on J.D.'s window and, when he rolled the window down, handed through two cups of coffee and a brown paper bag.

Quinn quirked an eyebrow. "So you brought breakfast but didn't want to arm me with hot coffee until I'd read the bad news."

J.D. shrugged as he peeked into the bag. "Didn't know how you would react. No doughnuts. Two muffins. Looks like blueberry."

Quinn took the proffered muffin. And then said, by way of thanks, "I can handle a little bad news. I don't need to be coddled like a damn schoolgirl."

J.D. nodded, but—Quinn noticed—didn't apologize. Instead he said, "If that were my woman in there—" he nodded toward the house "—and I had to go in and tell her what you just learned about her brother, I figure I might be too angry at the bastard to calmly sit here drinking coffee."

Quinn leveled a gaze at J.D. "Then it's a good thing she isn't my woman. Isn't it?"

In sheer defiance, he took a bite of the muffin and chewed in silence. Slowly. And calmly. To make sure J.D. didn't misinterpret his chewing as anger.

He didn't want J.D. thinking he needed to be protected. The best protection there was would be getting information as soon as it was available, not when someone else thought he was ready to hear it. His feigned indifference had nothing to do with how he felt about every damn person in the company knowing his business.

Because of course he was angry. If it were up to him, he'd hunt Corbin down and rip the bastard a new one. Quinn only wished his motives were pure. That he wanted to find Corbin because the man had broken the law. Or because he may have done irreparable damage to McCain Security's reputation. Or even because his actions would break Evie's heart. No, right now Quinn despised Corbin for the simple reason that Corbin had probably just destroyed any chance Quinn had of winning Evie back.

Because Quinn would hunt Corbin down. And Quinn would turn him over to the authorities. He had to do it. Because it was his job and it was the right thing to do. But once he'd done it, Evie would never forgive him.

So instead of doing what he should do—which was march up to Evie's doorstep and question her again—Quinn sat there eating his muffin and sipping his coffee as if his heart hadn't just been ripped out of his chest.

He was choking down another flaky bite of muffin when there was another knock on the window. He looked up, expecting to see Alyssa again. Instead, it was Evie.

She stood shivering in a knobby cream sweater and a pair of wide-legged pants that looked far too thin for the cold. Her arms were wrapped around her waist, which—combined with the dark circles under her eyes—made her appear more drawn and frail than he knew her to be.

J.D. rolled down the window, looking sheepish as he said, "Can I help you, ma'am?"

Evie crouched to talk through the open window. "Let's have it," she said.

"Have what?" J.D. sipped his coffee in a fair imitation of innocence.

"Whatever news you have." She shifted her gaze pointedly from Quinn's car to the one behind it. "Obviously you had something to report or you wouldn't be out here at six in the morning. If I get any more cop cars out here, my neighbors are going to start thinking I'm selling crack out of the back bedroom."

"We're not police offi—"

"Whatever," she snapped. "Neither of you blend well with the neighborhood." She rolled her eyes in Quinn's direction. "Give that one a cape and people would mistake him for Captain America. Now tell me what you know."

Quinn knew what she was really asking. She'd bid him not to come to her with evidence; she wanted proof. She didn't want to know what he'd found out. She wanted to know if he had proof yet. He managed to choke down his turbulent emotions and finally meet Evie's eyes. "Go back inside. I'll be in in a minute."

She held his gaze for a long time. Her green eyes were filled with concern, her face lined with exhaustion.

Eventually, she nodded, turned and headed back for the house, muttering something about coffee.

As Quinn and J.D. climbed out of the car, J.D. asked, "So you want me to stay here?"

"No. Go back to the office. Let me know if you hear anything more from the FBI. But don't share what you've found out with them for at least another day or so. We'll just have to hope they're confident enough with their own investigation that they don't come to us for information before then."

"And if they do?"

"Then give them the file. I don't want to be accused of obstructing justice." As he rounded the car and headed up Evie's walkway, he added, "And make sure the jet is gassed up and the pilot's ready to go."

J.D. nodded his understanding. "Flight plan?"

"Cayman Islands. As soon as possible," he said grimly. "I'm going to go down there, find the bastard and drag him back."

But first, he'd have to face Evie and decide whether or not to tell her the truth about her brother.

Evie felt as if she hadn't slept at all. Her eyelids burned as if they were lined with sandpaper, her throat was dry and swollen as if she'd been up all night crying, when in fact, she'd just been up most of the night trying not to cry. When she had slept, she'd drifted in and out, dreaming over and over again that she and Quinn were driving down that dark country road, the police lights flashing behind them. Except in the dream the person who pulled Quinn from the car wasn't Sheriff Moroney but Corbin. And then an FBI agent would appear and arrest her and throw her in jail. And each time as she was pulled away and stuffed into the cop car, Quinn just stared at her with his impassive gaze void of emotion.

She was losing him all over again. Not that she'd *had* him. Not that she'd necessarily *wanted* him. But for a few minutes last night, there seemed the possibility that she might one day earn his trust again. And during those few heady moments, her heart had soared.

After the evening and the night she'd had, she wasn't up to contemplating what that meant for her emotionally. All she knew was that just now, when she'd gone out to his car, the look Quinn gave her said it clearly enough: Corbin was in a whole big heap of trouble. And Quinn— being Quinn—was going to treat this mess with his unquestioning sense of honor.

"Oh, for goodness' sake, it should not be this difficult!" She threw down the coffee scoop in her frustration.

"Do you need help with that?"

She jumped at the sound of Quinn's voice, startled to see him standing in the doorway to her kitchen.

"What?" Then she noticed he was looking from her to the coffeemaker with an expression of mild confusion on his face. If only all her frustrations in life could be blamed on Mr. Coffee, not the inscrutability of men. "Oh," she muttered dumbly, picking the scoop back up and resuming the task. "No. I've got it. I assume I'm going to need caffeine for this."

Quinn's lack of response was answer enough. She watched him, waiting for him to cross the tiny kitchen and pull her into his arms. To offer her the solace of his embrace, even if the news he had to share would bring no comfort at all. But he didn't move toward her, and with each passing second the gap between them seemed to grow wider.

Quinn scowled. He stood with his hip propped against the cabinet and with his hands curled around the edge of the counter. "Evie, about your brother…"

His hesitancy surprised her. The Quinn she knew from high school had always been slow to speak, thinking everything through before opening his mouth. But so far, Quinn the adult was none of those things. He was passionate, decisive, angry, disdainful even. But cautious wasn't anywhere on the page.

"Yes," she prodded, clutching the handle of her empty coffee mug.

"Tell me how you first found out he owed money to the Mendoza brothers."

"It was…I don't know, a couple of weeks ago, I guess." Her brain was sluggish, on top of feeling jittery. To help clear her thoughts, she turned back to the coffeemaker and pulled the carafe out to pour herself a cup mid-brew. "Corbin started acting strangely. Nervous all the time. I knew something was up. I questioned him until he caved."

"What exactly did he tell you?"

"Not much," she admitted, adding a generous dose of sugar to the mug. "Just that he owed some people a lot of money. That he'd been gambling again and that he'd lost badly."

"Again?" Quinn asked.

"When he first got out of college, he floundered for a bit," she admitted ruefully. "Dad supported him for a year, but then cut him off. Insisted he find a job or go back to school for his master's. Since Corbin wasn't interested in either, he started gambling professionally."

"Professionally?"

"I don't know." Her cheeks flushed, not liking to admit that she purposefully turned a blind eye to her brother's behavior. "I assumed it was like poker tournaments and that kind of thing. Like you see on TV. I think he thought it was glamorous."

"And he made a living at this?"

"Not a very good one." Quinn seemed to be eyeing her mug, so she busied herself fixing him a cup of coffee, sipping her own between sentences. "He borrowed money a lot. But then after a few months, things settled down. He started doing better, I suppose. He stopped talking about it. Didn't borrow money for a long time. I just assumed he was doing okay."

She handed Quinn the cup of coffee and laughed nervously. "More than okay," she admitted. "He moved from one condo to the next, each one more tony than the last. His clothes got nicer. His cars faster." She didn't want to admit that she'd ignored his spending. Pretended how he made his money wasn't her business. "Obviously I should have paid more attention."

"Your brother is a grown man. You're not responsible for this mess he's in."

She smiled wryly at Quinn's attempt to comfort her, even as she wondered if he really believed it himself. He might be willing to make excuses for her, but that didn't necessarily translate into forgiving her for her part in this.

"So he finally broke down and told you about the gambling debt…" Quinn prodded.

Was that sarcasm in his voice when he said the words "broke down?"

"That was a couple of weeks ago. He was so upset. He didn't want my help," she insisted. "I had to beg him to let me help him find the money."

"I'm sure you did."

"He was humiliated at having to ask for help. But I told him I'd do anything. That I'd talk to our father. That I'd take out a loan. Anything." She shook her head. Clutching her mug in both hands, the heat from the coffee seeped through the ceramic, almost too hot to hold. But she clung to it anyway, needing the sting to keep her grounded.

"Whose idea was it to come to me?"

"It was my idea." Was this it? The reason he was being so cold? Did he hold her responsible for getting him into this mess?

"He didn't suggest it?" Quinn asked.

"No. I thought of it."

"Are you sure?"

"Yes." But suddenly she wasn't sure. Suddenly she desperately wanted him to hold her. But he stayed steadfastly on the other side of the kitchen. "I mean, I think so. Your name just came up in the conversation. Once it did, I just knew how to get the money he needed. He certainly didn't ask me to come to you." Which was all true, but thinking back, she couldn't remember which of them had mentioned Quinn's name first.

But of course, it had to have been Corbin, didn't it? She never mentioned Quinn. Never thought about him. Never let even the barest hint of him creep into her mind for fear he'd take up residence there. That her longing for him would nestle in deep. Burrow into her soul and she'd never banish it again.

But she couldn't think about any of that now. Because Quinn was here, in front of her, impossible to ignore. And she was in more trouble than she ever dreamed possible. Not just her heart was in danger, but her brother's future, as well. And that needed to be dealt with before she could even consider what this all meant to her emotional health.

"Please," she all but begged. "No more questions. Just tell me what you've found out."

After a moment more of studying her, he nodded. "So far it looks like there was only one person responsible for the actual theft—that is, the person who cracked the safe and physically removed the diamonds from the premises."

The dread that had been simmering in her belly for the past week finally reached boiling point. She sank to a nearby chair at the table. She knew what he was going to say. Still he kept talking, laying out all the details.

Giving it to her straight. Just like she'd begged him to do.

"The FBI thinks he hired on with the catering staff. Maybe weeks ago."

Quinn very carefully hadn't mentioned her brother's name yet, she noticed. But was still talking about him in the form of some mysterious unidentified "him." But she knew who Quinn meant. They both knew.

But she had asked Quinn not to tell her anything until he had proof. Apparently he was taking her at her word. As if by not mentioning Corbin's name, Quinn would protect Evie.

"He was with the catering crew through the initial setup in the afternoon. It's how he got access to the office. There must have been someone working elsewhere in the building to disable the security system because at some point he was able to slip away unnoticed from the rest of the staff. In the service hall used by the caterers, we believe he entered the ductwork and from there made his way up to Derek's office. Since it was a Saturday and everyone there was busy getting ready for the fundraiser, none of the Messina Diamonds staff was on that floor."

She wanted to ask about that security system. The one Quinn had sworn no one could break into. But her question would only sound accusatory and this wasn't his fault. Besides, she knew Quinn well enough to know that he'd probably already taken on enough of the blame himself without her adding more to that. So she remained quiet.

"He must have cracked the safe and taken the diamonds before any of the guests even arrived. He had to leave through the ductwork, as well. Since the space was small and cramped, he'd have been covered in grime. He couldn't have returned to the catering job. He must have known that would happen ahead of time because he had someone disable the cameras on the eleventh floor, where he exited the ductwork, changed clothes and made his way out of the building when all the guests were arriving."

Her mind clung stubbornly to a single ray of hope. "The ductwork was small, you said. My brother's tall." Not as tall as Quinn, of course, but nearly five-eleven.

"He's tall, but he's lean."

Irrationally, she shot out of her chair, ready to defend him. "How do you know? You haven't seen Corbin since high school. He could be broad as a football player now."

"But he's not." Quinn slowly shook his head, as if disappointed in her defense of Corbin. Still, he flipped open the folder he held and withdrew an eight-by-ten black-and-white photo and handed it to her. "This is a blowup from the security camera in the catering area."

Despite the grainy quality of the picture, she could see that it was Corbin, dressed in a crisp white chef's jacket that looked impossibly big on him, emphasizing the narrowness of his shoulders and the leanness of his frame.

She sank back to her chair. "Oh, Corb, what have you done?"

Quinn lowered himself to the chair beside her and placed his hands over hers. "You're not responsible for this. Corbin made his own choices."

Funny, under any other circumstances, she'd be the one saying that. She said that exact same thing at work all the time. People make their own decisions. You can get them help when they ask for it, but you can't take responsibility for their mistakes. But this was her brother. Who she'd been taking care of since she was five. And she had found herself making the lame protests family members always made.

"You mentioned other people," she said. "The people who disabled the cameras and security system. What about them?"

"What about them?"

"Well, they're involved, too, right? What if you find Corbin first? Talk to him? Convince him to turn himself in so that he can cut some kind of deal with the government? You could do that, right?"

"That's not how it works."

"Sure it is. You see it all the time. The witness protection program and all that. People cut deals in exchange for testimony against a bigger fish. That would at least keep him out of prison, right?"

She was waiting, praying that Quinn would agree. But he carefully dodged her question. Instead he reached across the table and cupped her cheek with his other hand.

"I promise you this, Evie. I will find your brother. And I'll do it before the FBI does. If there's a deal to cut, I'll make it work."

And just like that he stood and made to leave. She dashed after him, catching up with him in the living room.

"Wait a second. Where are you going?"

"I'm going to find your brother."

"I'll come with you."

"Absolutely not."

She practically threw herself in front of the door, blocking his exit. "Yes, I will."

"No."

"Quinn, this is important. You've got to let me come. I can help. I can talk to him. I know I can."

After a minute, Quinn gave a tight nod. Her surge of relief was tempered by his next words. "But only if you've got a passport."

"Why on earth would I need a passport to go to my brother's condo?"

Even as she said the words, she realized her brother wouldn't be at his condo. He'd be hiding out somewhere. Quinn answered her next question before she even had a chance to ask it.

"He's not at his condo," Quinn said. "I believe he's already in the Cayman Islands."

Eight

The quiet decisiveness with which she accepted his pronouncement took him completely by surprise. She merely nodded, her expression set in lines of grim determination. "I'll go get my passport, but I don't think he'll be there."

Quinn tucked his hands into his pockets, his shoulders drooped, weighted down by her disbelief. "You don't have to come. I didn't ask you to."

She frowned, her conviction seeming to waver. "It's not that I don't trust you."

His lips curved in a wry smile. "Obviously."

"But my brother is the only family I have left. And I'm the only family he's got, as well. Someone has to believe in him."

She might as well have kicked him in the gut. Once, she'd believed in him like that. All that glorious faith could have been his. And he'd thrown it away.

If she didn't want him touching her now, that was his fault. Things could have been different. But now the only solace he could offer was the comfort of knowing that he'd find her brother before the Feds did.

When he nodded his understanding, she propelled herself across the room and into his arms. He held her close, wanting to be the strength and comfort that no one else in her life was.

His hand was at the back of her head, stroking her hair in slow even motions. "You should stay here. Rest for a few days. Take it easy. I'll let you know if I find anything."

If I find anything, he'd said.

But, of course, what he meant was when I find Corbin.

He could tell she was tempted. She could stay here. Let her life just go on. Go back to work on Monday. Bury herself in the problems of other people. Pretend her brother wasn't in serious trouble. Pretend he hadn't involved her—however unwillingly—in something illegal.

Quinn prayed that she'd agree. Like everyone else in her life, he, too, had failed her. But he could take on this burden for her. He could find her brother. Bring him safely home, even if it was to face the consequences of his actions.

Quinn knew she may never forgive him for the part he would have to play in this, but at the very least, she didn't have to be on hand to see her brother come to justice.

But of course, Quinn knew she wouldn't let him handle everything for her. She wasn't the type to back down from things, no matter how unpleasant they might be. She'd always prided herself in being as tough as they came. Whatever happened with her brother, she'd face it head-on.

She pulled herself away from the shelter of his arms.

"Okay, I'll go pack."

"I'll be back in an hour to pick you up, if you're sure," he said as he headed for the door.

"Yes, I'm sure. I can't let you do this for me."

He hesitated, his hand already on the doorknob. "I need you to understand, I'm not doing this only for you. I owe Messina Diamonds everything I have."

"I know." She nodded, a sad little smile playing about her lips. "And your business is everything to you. I understand. I don't expect—" She blew out a breath. "Well, no matter what happens, I know where your priorities lie."

Unable to stand the sheer vulnerability in her gaze any longer, he simply left. Maybe the time apart would do them both good.

Quinn figured there was a decent chance that he'd strangle Corbin if he ever got close enough to wrap his hands around the other man's throat. And chances were pretty good he'd be able to convince a court the idiot had it coming. Even if Quinn wasn't able to defend his actions, it'd still be worth it.

Sitting beside Evie in the back of the limo he'd hired

to pick them up, he couldn't help noticing how the past few days had worn on her. Her face was drawn and pale. She had dark circles under her eyes that she'd been either unwilling or unable to hide with makeup. She'd pulled her hair back into a simple barrette, but several strands hung loose, not in an artfully enticing way. In fact, it rather looked as if she'd clipped her hair back while doing something else—packing, probably—just to get it out of her eyes, and had then forgotten she'd done it.

The difference between how she looked today and how she'd looked on Wednesday was marked. That day she'd obviously made an effort to look her best. Today she'd made no such effort. Not that he minded. To him, she was lovely no matter how she dressed. No matter how exhausted she was.

No, he minded because she deserved better than this. She deserved to have a family that loved her. Not a father that had—for all intents and purposes—abandoned her and a brother who used her for his own gain.

"You don't have to come," he said again.

"Yes, I do. I want to," she insisted. She said it without turning her attention from her purse, which she'd been nervously thumbing through ever since she'd gotten into the car. "I've got a neighbor checking on the pets while I'm gone. I have my wallet and my passport," she muttered. "Those are the most important things. Anything else I've forgotten I can buy when we get there, right?"

Still babbling nervously, she didn't wait for him to answer before pulling out her wallet and fingering the edges of two credit cards where they sat nestled in slots. "I should have more than enough room on this card. It's my emergency card, but I've never bought a ticket last minute like this. How expensive do you think it'll be? I've got a five-thousand-dollar limit. Will that cover it?"

"You're not paying."

"Of course I'm paying. I always pay my own way."

"Not this time." It was the least he could freakin' do. He was not letting her pay her own way when she tagged along to help him arrest her brother.

Not that he had the jurisdiction to actually arrest Corbin when they found him. Even the FBI would have had to work with local authorities and have him extradited. No, right now Quinn was focusing on finding him, getting the diamonds back and encouraging him to return to the States. The thought of Evie having to witness any or all of that made Quinn's gut clench in knots.

"I'm certainly not letting you pay."

She said it with such fierce defensiveness that he instantly felt like a cad. Such pride and independence. Here she was, all ready to whip out her five-thousand-dollar-limit credit card.

"Are you always this proud, or is it me you don't want to accept handouts from?"

She clenched her jaw as a blush flooded her cheeks. "I don't accept handouts from anyone."

But she'd waited a little too long to say it. So while that might be true in general, he could tell she was being particularly vigilant when it came to him. Fair enough. He'd been on the other end of this conversation enough times. Doing without was bad enough. Feeling like the object of pity only made it worse.

Still he'd never been on this side of the conversation before. He'd never been in the position of wanting to help and having no means of doing so without stomping all over someone else's pride.

"If it makes you feel better, you can handle your own incidentals once we get there. But you can't pay for your own plane fare. We're taking a private jet."

She stared at him blankly as his words sank in. "A private jet?" she finally repeated. "You rented a jet for this?"

As she asked the question, the limo pulled off the tollway and turned toward Love Field, the smaller of Dallas's two airports.

"I didn't rent the jet. It's a company jet."

"Owned by Messina Diamonds or McCain Security?"

"By McCain."

"Great. It's your jet." She spoke through gritted teeth. "You own a jet."

"It's a company jet," he repeated.

"Right. Which I'm sure you need to jet off to all your exotic international locations." She waved a hand dismissively, as if she wasn't bothered by the discussion, when obviously she was. "So half of the cost of taking a private jet to the Cayman Islands is…" She did a few exaggerated computations on her fingers. "Oh, let's see, that figures out to be about, my annual salary. What do you think, is that about right?"

"So you can't pay for your airfare. It's no big deal."

"It's no big deal to you," she said pointedly, as if money were the issue between them.

"Hey." He gently nudged her chin up so she was forced to meet his gaze. "You always said money wasn't important. That it would never stand between us." She'd said it over and over again when they were dating back in high school. Since he'd had no money to spend, he'd had no choice but to take her at her word. "Did you really believe that?"

"Of course I did!" Indignation flashed across her face.

"Then what's different now? If money doesn't matter, it shouldn't matter if it's my money or yours."

He couldn't count the times he'd had to swallow his pride and let her pay for something because she'd literally had to pay for everything. His meager salary from Mann's had covered living expenses for him and his father. Not movie tickets, not burgers at the local drive-through, not flowers on Valentine's Day. At seventeen, that one had killed him.

"That was different." Her tone was short and she wouldn't quite meet his gaze.

"Different how? Because then you were the one with money instead of me? Because now you're the one needing help?"

"No." She glared at him. "Because we were a couple then. We were dating. It's one thing to accept help from someone you're in love with, it's—"

Then she floundered, clearly not knowing how to finish the sentence. But he could guess what it was she didn't want to say aloud. It was something else entirely to accept help from someone you *weren't* in love with.

She frowned, an expression that could have been either guilt or doubt. He no longer knew her well enough to know which.

"Quinn, I—"

"I understand." He released her and shifted to face the front of the limo. "Things are different between us now. But there's nothing I can do about the jet. It's ready to go. We couldn't get a commercial flight for hours and time is of the essence."

She gave a tight nod. "I'll—"

"And don't tell me you'll pay me back." His words came out curter than he intended. But, jeez, what was he supposed to say?

A moment later the limo pulled up on the tarmac. As soon as they were settled on the plane, she opened her mouth as if she wanted to say more, but he cut her off.

"You're exhausted," he reminded her. "Try to get some sleep on the plane. It's about a four-hour flight."

Once they got to the island, there'd be enough time and privacy there for her to tell him in more detail about how she didn't love him anymore. Not that he had thought she did love him. He just hadn't known it would hurt so much to find out she didn't.

Evie was sure she'd never sleep under the circumstances. Despite that, she fell asleep curled up on one of the luxuriant leather seats not long after takeoff. She blamed the chair itself, which was more cozy than her decade-old mattress. The comfortable seat, combined with the white noise of the plane, lulled her to sleep.

She woke a few hours later to see Quinn still seated in one of the chairs on the opposite side of the plane, Bluetooth headset on. He was simultaneously talking on the phone in a hushed voice while typing on his laptop.

She could see nothing out the window except the bright blue ocean and a scattering of clouds. Quinn was so busy working he didn't notice she'd woken, so she took the opportunity to watch him unobserved. When they'd first gotten on the plane, she'd used the restroom. She'd been unable to ignore how worn her reflection had looked in the mirror. Though she'd managed some quick repairs to her hair, she could only hope the sleep she'd gotten just now had moved her appearance from scary to presentable.

Naturally Quinn looked fantastic. He wore a charcoal-gray suit that seemed as though it had been tailored to fit his broad shoulders. For all she knew, it actually had been. His face bore signs of concern just like hers did, but the lines made him appear more rugged than haggard.

Before she could get overly depressed about that realization, Quinn stood and crossed the cabin to the seat next to her. As he buckled himself in, he said, "You look better. Did you sleep well?"

Feeling as emotionally raw as she was at the moment, she couldn't bear his kindness. So instead of answering, she said, "It looked like you were working. Have you learned anything new?"

"We'll be landing soon. There's no point in going over it until we're settled at the house."

"I'd rather—" she began.

But he ignored her. "Why don't you tell me how you got into social work."

Obviously he was trying—again—to change the subject. He didn't want to talk about her brother? Fine. That's what she'd asked for, right?

Of the four leather chairs facing each other, Quinn sat in the one catty-corner to hers. So she swiveled her chair to face his head-on. Tucking one leg up under the other, she asked him, "Why are you doing this?"

"Doing what?"

"Being so *nice*. So polite. As if I'm some sad little social obligation. Because you should know, it's seriously pissing me off."

His lips twitched and he looked as though he wanted to laugh. But there was still something sad in his gaze. Which, she noticed, pointedly wouldn't meet her own. Ah. So the polite behavior she found so annoying must be motivated by something she'd like even less.

She cringed. "Don't tell me you're doing this because you feel sorry for me."

"I don't pity you." His tone was firm, but there was something else in his gaze.

She cocked her head to one side and studied his expression, trying to pin down exactly what that was she saw in his eyes. "No, you don't pity me," she murmured. "It's something else." And he wouldn't quite meet her gaze. Her own emotions went sour in her stomach. "It's guilt." Blecch. That was almost as bad as pity. "But what do you possibly have to feel guilty about? Your father didn't try to throw me in jail."

"Evie." He leaned forward a little. And despite what she'd said earlier, there was a tinge of pity in his gaze. "I know your life didn't turn out exactly as you planned."

She recoiled back in her chair. "My life?"

"You were going to travel. To backpack across Europe. You wanted to live in New York City and work in the fashion industry. Instead you and you father had a falling-out over me. You had to pay your own way through college. You even went to community college for a year."

Which he couldn't have possibly known unless he'd been digging around in her personal information. Not that she didn't see that coming. After all, he ran a security company. Undoubtedly he had that kind of information at his fingertips. Plus, he'd already told her he'd looked into her finances. Still, it felt underhanded.

She turned to stare out the airplane window to hide her emotions. "I suppose you know every move I've made since you left Mason."

"No. Not every move. Just enough to wonder how you ended up here."

For a moment, she considered pulling one of his tricks and avoiding the question. But if he was motivated by guilt, then she wanted to nip this in the bud. "It was because of your father, actually."

"*My* father?"

The surprise in his voice snagged her attention, so she turned her gaze from the view out the window back to him. Confusion was writ clearly on his face. So, he really didn't know everything she'd done.

"After you left Mason, I floundered for a bit." She'd stormed and sulked and generally acted like a child. Frankly, she didn't know what else to do. Her father had won. "You were gone," she said aloud now. "And no one else in town seemed to even notice."

She hadn't been able to stand the smug, easy explanations people had for Quinn's absence. *"I always knew he'd leave once he got the chance,"* some people would say, which was the closest they'd ever come to complimenting Quinn. Other people said things like, *"Good riddance."* Or *"With a father like that, we're better off now that he's gone."*

"So I started spending time with the only other person in town who cared that you were gone."

"My father," he said grimly.

"Yes, your father." The expression of distaste that crossed his face was so profound, she almost laughed. Yet at the same time, she knew just what he was thinking. It was unimaginable that she, Evie Montgomery, had set a single well-manicured foot inside the trailer in which he'd grown up.

Well, it had been a surprise to her, too, the first time she'd done it. When Quinn had lived in town, he'd never let her get within a hundred yards of the place. The first time she'd visited his father, she'd understood why. Frankly, she was surprised the place hadn't been condemned years earlier. If there'd been any adult in town who'd cared about Quinn's well-being, it would have been.

"It wasn't that big of a deal. I stopped by once or twice a week. Made sure he had groceries. Deposited the checks you sent home from the army." His frown had turned into an outright scowl, so she said, "Look, I'm sure there's a reason why the thought of my helping your father really irritates the pee out of you, but I can't imagine what it is."

Instead of answering her, he said, "So those semesters you went to community college before going to Texas State…"

Ah. So he'd figured that out. "Yeah, I didn't leave Mason and go away to school until after your dad passed away," she admitted. "It didn't seem right to leave him without anyone to take care of him."

"It shouldn't have been you," he said quietly.

"Then who, Quinn? You?" She could see the guilt etching his face, but she wouldn't let him get buried under it. He had far too many regrets as it was.

And taking care of his father had been so *good* for her. It had pulled her out of her own grief. Given her something outside of herself to think about. Something beyond her own little world of smothering wealth and loneliness.

"You couldn't do it," she pointed out. "You'd had to leave town because of *me*. It seemed only fair that I be the one to take on your burdens. And, you know, I'm glad it was me instead of you. It was a lot easier for me to watch him drink himself to death than it would have been for you to."

"If I'd been there, maybe I would have—"

"Been able to stop him? It's not likely. Your father was what he was. An alcoholic with a death wish. He was on a path of self-destruction long before you left town. That was his choice. His. Not yours. You can't save everyone, Quinn."

"That's almost funny coming from you."

She stiffened. "What's that supposed to mean?"

"You were willing to sleep with me to get the money to save your brother."

"Oh, please." She waved a dismissive hand. "I would never have let it get that far and you're the last man on earth to follow through with a threat like that. And neither of us looks particularly good when we talk about that incident, so maybe we should take that off the table."

He nodded. "Fair enough. Still, you're the social worker. You save people for a living. And you just admitted to putting your life on hold back in high school so you could take care of my father, who you hated."

"I never hated your father," she admitted. "I hated that he was an awful father to you, but I never hated him as a person."

Quinn was silent for a long moment as he considered what she'd said. He scrubbed a hand along the back of his neck, a sure sign that her words bugged him, so she prodded, "Come on, Quinn, tell me what you're thinking."

He sent her an annoyed look. "Why don't you tell me what I'm supposed to be thinking? Because I don't know what to do with this."

"You're not supposed to *do* anything with this. I didn't help your father because I expected something from you in return."

"Then why did you do it?"

"Because he was your father. It was my fault he was all alone. I chose to take care of him. In the end, it was an experience I found rewarding, so I chose to do social work. Again, my choice. Not yours."

She gave him a pointed stare, waiting for him to respond. But he didn't. Instead, without meeting her gaze, he said, "It looks like we're about to land. You better make sure your seat belt is on."

And once again, he'd effectively ended the conversation. He was remarkably good at avoiding the things he didn't want to talk about. His father had always topped that list.

Well, she could sympathize; she didn't particularly want to talk about her family right now, either. Finally they were in agreement about something.

She spent the drive from the airport thinking of what to say to Quinn. He was silent as the car wound its way from the airport through town to an isolated stretch of beach dominated by a promontory jutting out over the ocean. The Queen Anne–style house where they were going to stay managed to look both impressive and historically quaint. Without another house around for miles, it looked like something out of the Caribbean-set gothic romances she'd read as a teenager. Was there a pirate ship moored just around the point? Or perhaps waiting in the house she'd find a brooding English lord, complete with a mad wife hidden in the attic.

Her musings might have amused her, if it hadn't been for the weight of Quinn's silence. Perhaps the image of the brooding lord was more apt than she thought. But did that make her the stupidly innocent young miss? Or worse, the mad wife in the attic?

She suppressed a giggle, feeling every inch the crazed Victorian lady. That kind of helplessness would drive her insane, too. If Quinn had any news about her brother, he wasn't sharing it.

By the time she'd gotten settled in one of the guest rooms, her stomach was twisted in knots. She left her hastily filled suitcase on the floor instead of unpacking it into the Bombay chest of drawers. She didn't plan on being here long enough for that.

She ignored the lure of the mosquito-netting-draped four-poster bed. If there was news of her brother—good or bad—she needed to know it. It was time she faced up to the truth.

Nine

Quinn was in the kitchen making a pot of coffee when Evie walked in. Besides the flat-screen TV dominating one wall of the living area, the kitchen, with its gleaming stainless steel appliances, was the one room of the house that looked as if it hadn't been transported right out of the Victorian age.

She looked as keyed up as she had on the plane. As though the strain from keeping her composure had worn her to the point of exhaustion. He should have fought harder to convince her to stay in Texas. Had he allowed her to come because he was giving in to her wishes or merely giving in to his own desire to have her near?

Either way, she was here now. And he'd keep her by his side as long as he could. He poured a mug of coffee and held it out to her, but she shook her head, opting instead to prop her hips against the butcher-block counter.

"You think he masterminded this whole thing, don't you?" There was a hint of accusation in her voice.

There were a dozen reasons why he believed exactly that. But the most convincing argument he could make was to say, "Occam's razor."

"No." She shook her head. "I don't believe it. I don't believe he's capable of this."

"It's the simplest explanation," he said as gently as he could.

He'd known this wouldn't be easy, but watching her expression, the worry lining her eyes and the tension framing her mouth, made it all harder than he'd thought it would be. Damn Corbin. He was the one who'd broken her heart. He should be the one here facing her now.

Yet even as he thought it, Quinn knew he would never give up his place by her side. As hard as it was to tell her the truth, he wouldn't dream of making her face it alone.

"Think about it," he said slowly. "You've been saying all along you couldn't believe he'd be this stupid. That he was smarter than this." Quinn nudged up her chin, forcing her to meet his gaze. "Maybe you were right. Maybe he was smarter. Smart enough to mastermind this whole thing.

"I asked around, found a contact working in the Mendozas' operation," he continued. "Yes, they have a hand in gambling, but they claim they've never loaned any money to your brother. He doesn't owe them fifty thousand dollars. He doesn't owe ten dollars."

"Why would he lie?"

This was the part that had taken Quinn the longest to figure out. The part that just hadn't made sense until he'd read the file J.D. had brought him in the car that morning.

Instead of answering her outright, Quinn pulled out his iPhone and pulled up a picture. "I want you to look at this picture. See if you recognize this man."

The guy in the picture was about her brother's age, maybe a year or two younger. He was dressed in the sort of expensively scruffy clothes that seemed endlessly popular with men in their twenties. His hair was shaggy, but he probably paid a lot to get it to look that way. In the photo he was sitting on a restaurant patio across from her brother. Corbin had on a gimme cap and sunglasses, not unheard of when sitting outside in the sun.

"Yes. That's Brent… No, Brett something. Patterson, maybe?"

"Brett Parsons."

"Right. My brother knew him at SMU. They were frat brothers or something. I only met him a handful of times. I never liked him. He was one of those rich kids who took six or seven years to get a degree."

Which must have been hard for her to deal with when she was struggling to make ends meet on a state employee's salary—not to mention dealing with poverty and social injustice every day—to watch some of her brother's wealthier friends fritter away fortunes.

"If I remember right, he was from money," she continued. "Back east. I had the impression he was spoiled and self-indulgent." She looked up at Quinn. "You wouldn't be showing me his picture if he wasn't involved. Can I assume my brother dragged him into this?"

"Don't feel too badly for him." Quinn clicked the phone into standby mode and slipped it back into his pocket. "*He's* the one who owes money to the Mendozas."

"So he's the gambler."

"And he's also the inside man."

Her gaze shot up to Quinn's. "The inside man?"

Quinn smiled a bit ruefully. "You can at least reassure yourself that you weren't the only one taken in here."

"He works for you?"

"No. He got a job at Messina Diamonds about four years ago working in Research and Exploration. However, McCain does background checks on all Messina employees. We'll be updating those protocols."

J.D. had been thoroughly chagrined to admit that he remembered doing the background check on Parsons himself. But four years ago, there'd been nothing there to raise a flag. Now, the guy had more debt than a third world country.

Evie studied Quinn for a minute. "But you don't think this guy planned it, do you? You think Corbin's behind everything."

Quinn watched her with a steady gaze. "I do. From what I learned about Parsons, he's desperate but not imaginative. I think your brother found his weakness and exploited it. Maybe even encouraged it. He—"

But Quinn broke off. Did she really need to hear all

of this? What good would it do to destroy the last of her faith in her brother?

"He, what?" she demanded. "I'd rather know it all. Whatever it is, finding out later isn't going to make hearing it any easier."

"Parsons wasn't the only one my contact with the Mendozas was able to inform me about."

"Tell me," she urged, her gaze earnest, her mouth pressed into a thin line of resolve.

"Your brother doesn't owe them any money, but the Mendozas are familiar with him. He doesn't do business with them, but apparently they keep tabs on pretty much all the lowlifes in the area. Frankly, they have better info than my source at the FBI."

"Lowlifes," she said with a humorless laugh. "And that includes my brother?"

"So far, it's mostly low-level con jobs. Nothing that interferes with their business. But he's been doing this kind of thing for years."

She wrapped her arms around her waist, looking cold. A storm front was moving in off the coast and the temperature had dropped a few degrees just in the time since their plane had landed. But Quinn doubted that was why she was suddenly trembling.

"So, my brother is a con man." As if trying to distract herself, she pulled a tumbler from the cabinet and filled it with water from the jug in the fridge. "And you think he was the mastermind of the robbery."

"I do. This guy, Brett Parsons, is the one who disabled the security system. His fingerprints are all over it. Metaphorically speaking. There was no way he was ever going to walk away from this. He was picked up about four hours ago trying to catch a flight to Cabo San Lucas."

"Four hours? So that's the news you got on the plane?"

Quinn nodded. "It is. He started talking right away. Frankly the FBI are having trouble getting him to stop talking. Since then, they've picked up five other guys that Brett has fingered, all of whom were either on their way to Mexico or already in Mexico waiting to be contacted by your brother. There's a resort on the Pacific coast with a reservation in Corbin's name. Airline tickets put him arriving there later this evening."

"Then why are we *here?*" she asked.

"Because he's not going to Mexico. He's probably not planning on ever returning to the States. The reservation and the airline ticket are just covers. He got me involved to ensure everyone else would be caught. Ten million dollars split five or six ways is a lot less money than if one person gets all of it."

He could see in her eyes the quiet struggle not to believe him. She didn't want to be swayed by his logic. She didn't want him violating her steadfast trust in her brother. Once again, Quinn fought that ache in his chest. She deserved to have someone in her life that she could trust. That someone should have been him. If only he'd had more faith in her. If he'd had half the faith in her that she had in her brother, how different might their lives have been?

"So he's betrayed his friends as well as me? I can't believe that. My brother is not that guy."

"Evie, I'm sorry—"

"He wouldn't do that. Not to me. You can't imagine the sacrifices I've made for him. I went to my father and begged for him. *Begged*. He wouldn't have let me do that unless…" Her voice broke. "You don't know him."

"Maybe. Or maybe it's you who doesn't know him."

As if she suddenly couldn't take it anymore, she turned and ran out of the house, toward the beach and the endless ocean beyond. Away from him.

He watched as she reached the sand and kicked off her shoes to walk barefooted into the tumbling surf. She stood there for a long time, with the waves licking her toes, her arms wrapped around her body as the wind whipped her hair around her face.

His resolve to leave her be, to give her time, to wait for her to come back to him, wavered as he watched her. He waited as long as he could, until the wind picked up and the clouds darkening the horizon turned charcoal-gray. A storm was coming and she wasn't prepared for the cold.

He grabbed a sweater out of the closet by the door and headed after her. He made it almost all the way to her before she heard his approach and turned to face him with her arms held like a defensive shield over her chest and her eyes blazing. The softness and vulnerability of their earlier conversation were gone. Before him was the girl he'd fallen in love with all those years ago. Proud, rebellious and too stubborn to back down from any fight.

Especially when it came to protecting the people she loved.

Had she looked this way back in high school when she'd faced down her father in his defense? Had she been this fierce in her protection of him? He wanted to believe she had.

Her voice didn't waver at all when she said, "I've always believed people should be allowed to make their own decisions. I just never dreamed Corbin would make such bad choices."

"Bull."

Her gaze snapped to his. "What?"

"You've always thought you should be allowed to make your own decisions. And you've always thought everyone else should do what you think is best."

"But—" she sputtered. "That's not tr—"

"Yes. It is true." He couldn't resist reaching out a hand to tuck a stray strand of hair behind her ear. "It's not a bad thing, wanting to protect the people you love."

"It is when they turn out to be criminals." Her eyes filled with tears. "How was I so wrong about him?"

"You love him, that's how."

And no doubt if Corbin was arrested, indicted and convicted with a mountain of evidence, she'd still be by his side, fighting for him. Her unblinking defense of the weak and helpless was undoubtedly what made her great at her job. It was one of the qualities that he admired most.

What would it be like to have someone who believed in him that much? Someone that devoted to him?

Of course, he'd had that with her years ago. How had

he ever walked away from her? Why on earth hadn't he trusted her?

"You know, when I went to see you last Wednesday," she said, interrupting his musing, "I was so sure you were holding on to the past. It was obvious to me that you'd never gotten over what had happened. I actually felt sorry for you." She let out a bark of wry laughter. "Because I'd moved on and you hadn't. I was so smug."

Listening to her talk about pitying him, he felt none of the resentment he normally would have. Instead he felt a gut-deep dread for what she was about to say.

"But really, what happened between you and I all those years ago affected me just as much as it did you. I just wasn't willing to admit it. I've been stubbornly clinging to this resolve to always think the best of everyone. To always give people the benefit of the doubt."

"Evie, your faith in others isn't a bad thing." He reached out a hand to her. "I could still be wrong about Corbin," he offered, even though he didn't really believe it.

But she shook her head. "No. I knew you were right about him when you explained how he got you involved to insure everyone else would be caught. Only Corbin would do something that damn cocky. Turns out he was playing everyone." She laughed. "I just wish I hadn't been such an easy mark. You must think I'm an idiot."

"I don't."

Life had kicked her in the teeth over and over and she still had the capacity to see the best in others. She wasn't naive the way he'd once accused her of being. She was resilient. It was one of the things he loved best about her.

There. He'd admitted it. To himself at least. He loved her. Maybe he'd never stopped loving her. Would he ever convince her to give him another chance?

"I don't want to argue about your brother." Goodness knew they would have enough of that in their future. He held out the sweater. "I thought you might be cold."

She bumped her chin up and refused to take the sweater from him. "I'm not."

"You're shivering."

"It must be the anger," she said defiantly.

"Or the fact that it's dropped fifteen degrees in the past hour."

She was clenching her jaw, and he couldn't tell if it was to stop her teeth from chattering or to keep back some venomous retort. Instead of arguing with her, he just draped the cardigan over her shoulders. Whoever the sweater belonged to was big enough that it enveloped her small frame. She continued to glare at him, not bothering to button the front or pull it closed around her.

Finally he reached to pull her into his arms, rubbing his hands up and down her chilled skin. After a moment of resistance, she melted against him. All that tremendous strength of will spilled over the edges of her like the waves lapping at their feet.

Her head sank to his chest as her arms crept around his waist. Fluttering in the wind, the ends of her hair brushed against his cheeks and tickled his nose. The sweet, spicy scent of her mingled with the crisp salt air, seeming both familiar and incredibly exotic.

She tipped her chin up, boldly meeting his gaze. Desire arched between them. He leaned down to kiss her, but the instant before his lips touched hers, she pressed her fingertips to his mouth.

"If you're just going to kiss me and walk away again, don't bother. I'm tired of being jerked around."

He had to smile at her cheek. "I didn't mean to jerk you around. I didn't want to take advantage of your emotional vulnerability. I thought I was doing the right thing."

"Well, it's damn irritating. If you don't want to sleep with me, fine. But don't be a tease."

She was probably the only woman in the world who would accuse him of that. He supposed it was only natural. After all, she was the only woman in the world who he cared enough about to try to protect from himself.

"I wasn't meaning to be a tease. I was only trying to protect you."

"I'm not a child. I don't need protecting."

She threaded her fingers around the back of his neck, toying with the close-cropped hair. It was a gesture of mindless affection, given with a casual disregard for how he might interpret it.

Maybe they had a shot at making this work, maybe they didn't. Either way, he was already a goner. She may not know it, but she held his heart in her hands. He had no defenses against her. And he didn't want any. When his mouth found hers, she met him willingly. She arched against him, pouring into the kiss the full range of her emotions. He tasted the sweetness of her yearning edged with the tang of her resentment. The lingering tartness of her anger mingled with the honeyed spice of lust.

She met him touch for touch. Her tongue rubbing against his even as her hands clutched at his clothes. She pulled his shirt free from his pants just as he slid a hand under the hem of her tank top. The heat of her skin under his palm was in sharp contrast to the breeze. Her own hands were cool but greedy as they brushed his nipples, stroked his shoulders, clung to his arms.

Her touch—her neediness—stirred his hunger like nothing else ever had. Desire was hot in his veins, pressing hard against the last of his restraint.

Still he tried to pull back from her, to tug her toward the house. Because they were outside, for Christ's sake. She deserved better than this. Deserved more than fast sex on the beach. More than the uncertainty of coupling their bodies when so much still stood between them. Unresolved. Unspoken.

But when he tried to pull away from her, she held tight to his arms. "No," she said.

No gentle pleading for her—it was more of an order. A demand.

"Evie," he murmured, but still she shook her head.

Wrapping her hand around the back of his head, she held his gaze. Steady, hot, unwavering. "Just this once, forget that stupid honor of yours. Toss it out the window along with your blasted chivalry. Stop treating me like you think I should be treated and just give me what I want."

And with that, she shoved his shirt off his shoulders and reached for his belt buckle.

Evie didn't want to let Quinn go for the simple reason that she feared if she did, she'd never get him back again. Quinn had a way of doing that. Autocratically deciding what was best for her and then refusing to be swayed. It was why they'd both been virgins that fateful wedding night all those years ago. Because he'd decided they should wait. It was undoubtedly why they hadn't had sex last night. Because he was too damn noble for his own good. And far too noble for hers, either.

Just for tonight she wanted to shove aside all the other things in their lives. She wanted to forget all the things standing between them. She wanted to pretend it didn't matter that they had no future together. Because if she didn't do it now, she never would. And she couldn't imagine a world in which she'd never get to be with Quinn.

And so she lost herself in his touch. In the feeling of his mouth moving over hers. Of his skin, smooth and hot, under her palms. Of his hands on her breasts, unhooking her bra.

Desire coiled through her, heating her body like a primitive chant. More. More. Now.

She shrugged out of the sweater he'd draped over her shoulders, only vaguely aware of it hitting the ground at her feet. It was the first item of clothing to hit the ground, but not the last. Her tank top followed. Then his belt. His shoes. Her pants.

With each article of clothing, they worked their way up the beach, to drier land, moving in tiny steps, until they were both naked, panting. Desperation made her greedy. She dropped to her knees before him, eager to explore his body.

She cupped the length of him in her hand, running her thumb over the tip of his erection before circling the head with her tongue. She felt a shudder go through his body as she sucked his penis into her mouth. A surge of pure feminine pride crashed through her as elemental as the storm blowing through around them. She was strong. Powerful. She swallowed just once before he pulled himself from her mouth.

Before she could protest, he knelt before her, holding her body tight to his. He kissed her hard before pulling back just far enough to meet her gaze as he said, "You don't get to control everything."

She bucked her hips against his as she bit down on her lip. "Says who?"

His smile was gentle and teasing, despite the hunger in his gaze. "It's not nice not to share."

He pulled her onto his lap so she was straddling him, his chest still pressed against hers. His penis was pressed intimately against her, and with every rock of her hips, it rubbed her clitoris. The pressure mounted inside of her. With his mouth on hers and his hands massaging her breasts, her climax built steadily until it came crashing down around her.

Her body was still twitching and needy when he gently set her off of his lap.

She began to protest. "What the—"

But then she saw him reaching for his jeans, fumbling with his wallet. To her everlasting relief, he withdrew a condom. A second later he was back with her, spreading the sweater on the ground, lowering her to it and himself to her.

By the time his body finally plunged into hers, she felt as though she'd waited a lifetime to feel him inside of her. Like she'd been wanting him, needing him, endlessly, forever.

And then he was touching the deepest part of her. Pounding into her, relentless, unending, eternal, like the waves crashing onto the beach, like the heavy drops of rain finally falling to the ground. As dark and heavy as the storm clouds. As primitive as the wind and the elements. At last he was hers.

Ten

She woke in the bed she'd shared with Quinn, but without him by her side. Though she missed him, she didn't feel bereft because he'd been beside her all night long.

After they made love the first time, he'd carried her and their clothes back to the house. He'd brought her to her bedroom where he'd lavished her body with attention. Made luxuriant, voluptuous love to her in that netted concoction of a bed. Then they'd slept, with their bodies pressed together all night long.

He'd been there every time she'd awoken in the night. Their bodies moving as one, cradling, cupping, spooning. More intimate than anything else she'd ever experienced. The wedding night they'd never had. Not just the sex of it, but the familiarity of it. The closeness she'd never had with another person.

She rolled over in bed now, pulling his pillow to her and burying her face in it, inhaling the scent of him. Then she kicked off the sheet and thumped her feet against the bed, relishing the tingly, just-loved feel of her skin. The air was still thick with humidity, but a shaft of sunlight played across the hardwood floor, proof that the storm had passed. From the kitchen, she heard the rattling of pans and dishes, caught the faint whiff of coffee brewing.

Just as she was contemplating breakfast in bed, she heard voices. Not Quinn's voice, but the rumbling baritone of multiple men in conversation.

Jerking upright in bed, she clutched the sheet to her naked chest. Well, crap. That meant breakfast in bed was out of the question.

Who was here?

She dressed quickly, pulling on denim shorts and a sea-green tank top. Since it was still cooler than the Caribbean had any right to be, she shrugged into Quinn's white linen shirt and tied it around her waist.

Quinn wasn't in the kitchen, but nearly a half-dozen other men were. One was manning the cooktop, with a mound of eggs in one skillet and bacon in the other. Another was pouring out mugs of steaming coffee. A few more had set up laptops on the kitchen table, with cords streaming down to the floor and a wireless modem blinking from a plug.

J.D. was the only man she recognized, so she went straight to him. He nodded a greeting, then introduced her to everyone. She promptly forgot their names, but they were all McCain Security employees and all had that former-military vibe. He introduced her simply as "Quinn's ex." But he must have explained their relationship beforehand because the men accepted her presence with a minimum of curious gawking.

"Did I miss something? When did y'all get in?" she asked as J.D. pulled a plate from the cabinet and began loading it with eggs and toast.

"Early this morning."

J.D. held out the plate and she took it, more out of instinct than hunger. "Isn't this yours?" she asked.

"Nope. Yours." He shoved a fork into the eggs. "Rick and Jax were up in Canada. They flew down to Dallas last night and picked up the rest of us."

Only then did she ask, "Hey, where's Quinn?"

She'd been up for a good ten minutes now and had seen neither hide nor hair of him.

"Out," J.D. said simply. But he didn't meet her gaze.

"You mean he's out dealing with my brother." Suddenly the eggs tasted less yummy and buttery and more dry and powdery. She set the fork on the plate and nudged it away. Since J.D. didn't seem prepared to say anything more, she prodded. "I don't like being handled. Obviously you're here to take care of me while Quinn goes off to find my brother."

J.D. kept his face expressionless, but unless she was mistaken, the muscles in his arms were twitching.

"It's okay," she said, even though it really wasn't. "You can be honest. I'm not going to freak out or anything." Okay, that *probably* was true. She'd done all her freaking out last night. "I know Quinn's come down here to arrest my brother or whatever."

"Technically, we wouldn't be arresting him. We don't have that kind of jurisdiction, not even in the United States. We would just encourage him to return with us to the States, where we'd hand him over to the authorities."

"What I don't get," she continued, "is why there are this many of you to keep an eye on me. Did you bring too many people or something?"

"No." J.D. seemed to be speaking through clenched teeth. "This is how many people I brought."

"But that would mean Quinn went alone. That can't be right."

J.D. scrubbed a hand along the back of his neck. "It is."

She sank back against the chair and took another bite of her toast, chewing thoughtfully. So Quinn had found her brother and had gone to pick him up alone. The thought of the two men in her life facing each other down was unsettling.

Corbin wasn't a big man. Quinn, with all of his lean muscles and his linebacker-width shoulders, probably had sixty or seventy pounds on him. Easy.

Still it didn't make sense. "Quinn's not a reckless man," she said aloud. "Why would he go alone? Sure he's bigger than my brother, so he should be able to 'encourage' him into a car with relative ease. But there are so many variables. Why would he risk losing control of the situation? My brother could get away."

J.D. sipped his coffee with stony silence, but a scowl of disapproval had settled onto his face.

She studied him for a minute and then looked around the room again. Nervous energy buzzed in the air. In her line of work, she knew plenty of cops—sure they weren't always on the same side of a fight—but she'd worked with enough of them to know how they behaved. Knew the sort of quiet jitteriness that settled over them when something bad was about to go down. That's how this group of men felt now.

Pinning J.D. with a stare, she said, "You know something you aren't telling me. What is it?"

But if something bad had happened to Corbin, Quinn would have told her. He wouldn't have vanished early in the morning and left her here to be babysat by this bunch.

"What is it?" she prodded again. "What's going on here?"

Finally J.D. relented. "Quinn's not planning on bringing your brother in."

The answer was so unexpected it took her several beats for it to register. "That's ridiculous. Of course he is."

"No, he's not. His plan is to get the diamonds and let your brother walk."

"Did he tell you that?"

"He didn't have to." J.D. leaned forward, pinning her with a stare, and for the first time she noticed the glint of resentment in his gaze. "Before he left for Cayman, we had a plan." J.D. tapped the table with his forefinger. "Get the diamonds, get the guy, hand both over to the FBI. Everybody's a winner."

Everybody, that was, who wasn't in her family.

"Then we arrive this morning," J.D. continued, "and the plan's kiboshed."

He didn't say any more, but he didn't have to. Obviously it didn't take a genius to see that the change in plans had to do with her and the fact that she and Quinn had slept together.

"Look," she said. "Whatever's going on, it doesn't have anything to do with me."

"Of course it does," he interrupted. "Corbin's your brother. What other reason would Quinn have for letting him walk?"

"That's what I'm saying. There's no way Quinn's going to let Corbin go. It's not in his nature."

Quinn had a stronger sense of right and wrong than anyone she'd ever known. He'd been the victim of injustice too many times in his life—both as the son of the town drunkard and during his brief stint as her husband. Because of that, his ironclad code of ethics was completely unwavering.

"Letting a criminal walk away would be wrong." She leaned forward, bracing her hands on the table. "Quinn would never do that."

"Then you didn't ask him to do it?"

She threw up her hands in frustration. "Of course I didn't. Is that what you really think? That I came down here to talk Quinn out of finding my brother? Or, oh wait, maybe this is it. I came down here pretending to help Quinn, but what I was really doing was trying to distract him so Corbin could get away."

At her rant, J.D. looked a little relieved as well as a little chagrined. "I just assumed—"

"Well, you were wrong."

"I'm glad," he said with a grin.

"And you're wrong about Quinn, too. He'd never do something so completely against his nature."

"He would for you." He said it quietly, but with such complete confidence that for a moment she was shocked into silence.

She pushed herself to her feet. "Do you know where Quinn went?" she asked J.D.

The look he gave her was full of suspicion. She rolled her eyes. "Look, I'm just trying to help." When the suspicion didn't fade, she added with emphasis, "To help Quinn. If he lets Corbin walk away, he'll never forgive himself. And if he does it because he thinks that's what I want, then he'll never forgive me, either."

J.D.'s mouth curved into a smile. "Well, at least we agree on that." He stood then and turned to the rest of the men. "Pack it up, guys. We're heading out."

Not five minutes later they were loaded into a van and heading down the coast. She only hoped they'd make it in time.

Quinn had faced a lot of unpleasant situations in his life, and none of them had been even half as scary as this—a sunburned tourist, complete with floppy straw hat, zinc oxide smeared on his nose, and hiking socks under his sandals, sitting in the Cayman Airways terminal waiting for a flight to Cuba.

At this early hour, the airline had several flights scheduled back to back, so the terminal was packed with travelers nursing cups of coffee, reading papers and sitting with their backs against walls, legs outstretched before them. Every seat of the decades-old leather seating was taken.

The tourist Quinn was interested in sat next to a pretty blonde, college-aged girl who was either suffering from a hangover or faking it in hopes the guy would take a hint and leave her in peace.

"And I've always wanted to travel more," the guy was saying. "So after the divorce I figured, what the hell, I might as well…"

He looked up when Quinn stopped before him, letting his words trail off. But damn, he was good. He didn't so much as blink in recognition. And even Quinn had to admit, the transformation from stylish, urbane Corbin to geeky tourist was so complete, even he might have missed it.

Quinn held out a twenty to the college student. "Go buy yourself some coffee," he suggested.

She snatched the bill and scurried off, looking more than a little relieved to escape, even if it meant giving up one of the coveted seats.

Behind bottle-thick glasses, Corbin blinked rapidly as if warding off an allergy attack. Then he scratched his nose, smearing the white goop. "I don't suppose," he began in the same nasally tones he'd used with the girl, "that it'd do any good pretending I don't know who you are."

"And I don't suppose you're going to make this easy on either of us."

"I don't see why I should. Grand Cayman is a very peaceful place. And you have no authority here whatsoever. Now if you'd come with a posse of FBI agents and a warrant for my arrest, that would be different." Corbin shrugged. "But since I see only you, I assume you've only got a bunch of your army flunkies with you. Which means maybe you can bring me in, maybe you can't."

Between Corbin's feet sat a canvas duffel bag emblazoned with the logo of a brand of popular scuba diving gear. Small enough for Corbin to carry on. But dive gear was heavy and no one would think twice about a scrawny tourist straining to heft a bag of it around. And a little bit of heavy lifting would definitely be necessary, since ten million dollars worth of diamonds was a lot of stones.

"I don't want you. Just the bag." Quinn nodded to the green duffel. "Just the rocks."

Corbin studied Quinn, shifting automatically to tighten his hold on the duffel handle. "I wouldn't have pegged you as the type."

"To let a guilty man go?"

"To steal the diamonds for yourself, let me go, and claim you never found either." He gave a *c'est la vie* shrug as he adjusted the glasses. "Tell you what, why don't we split the diamonds and go our separate ways?"

"You're not in a position to bargain."

"Ah, but I must be or we wouldn't even be having this conversation. Obviously you're reluctant to bring me in. Possibly you don't have the manpower, but maybe it's something else. Whatever the reason, it gives me the advantage."

"Just give me the bag. I could have airport security here in less than a minute."

"You could." Corbin studied him. "But I'm guessing you won't. You'd get the diamonds, but you'd lose the girl."

The PA system announced a flight was about to board. Around the room people began shuffling bags and gathering their things.

Corbin shifted the shoulder strap of the bag from one hand to the other, preparing to stand. "Well, if you'll excuse me, this is my flight."

For a second, Quinn felt a rush of respect for Corbin. It took a hell of a lot of guts to walk around with ten million dollars worth of diamonds in a scuba bag slung over your shoulder.

Admiration aside, Quinn still wasn't going to let him walk off with the diamonds. Quinn snaked out a hand and grabbed Corbin's arm. "I'm not letting you go. I can't let you take the diamonds and I won't let you get away with what you've done to Evie."

Corbin smiled a slow, lazy smile. "Ah. So then I was right. She was always your greatest weakness." He pulled his arm free. "In that case, maybe you should be thanking me instead of trying to steal from me."

"Steal from you?" Quinn asked in disbelief.

"These are mine now." Corbin patted the bag. "You can't imagine how long it took to plan this. I worked on this for years. No way am I handing them over to you. And if you're going to take them from me, you're going to need something a little stronger than 'pretty please.'"

Quinn studied the other man for a long time, considering his options. Was he really ready to let the guy walk—with the diamonds—just to keep Evie happy?

If he apprehended Corbin and brought him back to the States, he'd go to prison for a long time. And Quinn would lose Evie forever.

On the other hand, that was about ten million dollars worth of stones in that bag Corbin was casually hefting over his shoulder. Which was a hell of a lot of money to let just walk away. And it wasn't just money. It was money belonging to his best friend. It was his company's reputation on the line. *Was he really going to risk all of that for Evie's happiness?*

He'd come here this morning telling himself as long as he got the diamonds back, he'd be okay with letting Corbin walk. That was the deal he made with himself. He'd let her brother go, if he handed over the stones. Now it looked like he'd get neither.

Quinn stood, ramming his hands into his pockets as he watched Corbin blend in with the crowd of tourists waiting to board the plane.

Yes. He was.

She meant more to him than any of that. Money was made and lost every day. Either his friendship with Derek would survive this or it wouldn't, but Quinn felt pretty sure it would. Evie, on the other hand, was one of a kind. She meant more to him than any other woman he'd ever known. And he wasn't about to lose her again.

Quinn turned, ready to make his way back out of the airline terminal, only to see Evie dashing through the crowd toward him.

She stopped just short of him, panting as if she'd run all the way from the security checkpoint. In her hand she clutched an airline ticket like the one he'd had to purchase to reach the boarding gate.

"Don't tell me we're too late!"

"What are you doing here?" Quinn got the question out just as J.D. came up behind her.

"Did we miss him?" he asked.

Evie ignored Quinn's question and stood on her tippy toes, straining to see over the milling people. "Do you see him? Is he here? Has he even been here?" Instead of waiting for Quinn to answer, she hopped onto the chair Quinn had been sitting in and used the added height to get a better look at the crowd. Then she pointed toward the gate. "J.D., there! They're taking his ticket right now. In the straw hat and the red print shirt."

J.D. dashed off toward the gate, several of McCain Security's other people following. Before she could dash off after them, Quinn snagged her arm and stopped her.

He caught her easily. She looked up at him, indignation ablaze in her eyes as she wiggled out of his grasp.

"I can't believe—" she swatted at his bicep "—you were willing to just get the diamonds back and let Corbin go. Of all the stupid, brainless—"

But then she paused mid-swat and looked around on the ground. "Wait a second. I don't see a bag. J.D. said it would be big." She framed out the approximate size of the bag. "And that it would be heavy." She narrowed her gaze at him. "Why don't I see a big, heavy bag anywhere?"

Near the gate, a scuffle had broken out. No doubt J.D. and the rest of the guys were taking down Corbin.

Evie went pale. "Dear lord, tell me you didn't let him leave *with* the diamonds."

"He called my bluff," Quinn admitted. He studied her then, taking in every nuance of her expression. Finally he nodded toward the gateway and commotion there. "You know what you've done, don't you? J.D.'s going to get the diamonds back, but your brother…"

"My brother's finally going to have to live up to his responsibilities. He got himself into this mess."

Before he could stop her, she marched off after her brother. Quinn followed a few steps behind her. By the time she reached the gate, J.D. had the duffel bag in hand. One of the other guys had Corbin's arms pinned behind his back. The other guys who'd come with them were speaking with airport security.

Quinn didn't want her to have to face her brother. Personally, he wanted to rip Corbin limb from limb just so she'd never have to deal with the guy again. But she kept telling him she didn't need him protecting her. So he backed off and let her confront Corbin on her own.

She stopped mere inches from her brother. Her whole body seemed to tremble with emotion. Quinn held his breath, waiting to see what she'd do. Part of him wanted her to haul off and punch Corbin. Another part hoped she'd burst into tears. Corbin's betrayal had damn near broken her and he should have to deal with that first-hand.

But Evie, being Evie, did neither. She just got right in Corbin's face and asked, "Corbin, how could you?"

Corbin flashed a raffish grin. "Do you want like a step-by-step description? 'Cause that would take a while and I'm not sure these fine gentlemen are willing to wait."

She blinked, obviously surprised by his cavalier atti-tude, though it didn't surprise Quinn.

"Then you admit you did it?"

"Come on, sis. You got to admit you're a little im-pressed."

Then she slapped him so hard across the cheek a speck of blood pooled at the corner of his mouth. "I guess that's a 'no' then."

"I worried myself sick over you. I went to our father and begged for you. Can you even imagine how hard that was for me?"

For an instant, doubt crossed Corbin's face and Quinn wondered if Corbin wasn't sorrier for what he'd done than Quinn gave him credit for. But Evie was so lost in her diatribe, she didn't seem to see it.

"And after all I did for you, you were just leaving." She gestured toward the plane still waiting on the tarmac. "You were just going to leave me alone. Without a word of explanation. You were just going to leave me alone."

Her voice cracked on the word *alone*. Quinn stepped

forward then, placing a hand on her shoulder. At his touch, some of her tension seeped away and she shifted her weight to lean against him infinitesimally.

Corbin flashed her another one of those shit-eater grins of his. His gaze darted to Quinn. "But I didn't leave you alone, now did I? That was the genius of the plan. Even you have to admit it was a nice touch."

Quinn heard a commotion from the far end of the airport, and glancing in that direction he could see some of the airport security guards rushing in their direction.

Evie must have seen them, too, because she asked quickly, "Why, Corbin? You're a smart guy. You could have done anything. Why be a thief?"

"It's what I do, sis. It's what I'm good at."

And then the security guards were there. Quinn quickly turned Evie into his chest so she wouldn't have to see them arrest her brother. He moved her away quickly. Whatever was going to happen, J.D. would handle it.

When they were far enough from the fray for privacy, she pulled herself from his arms and said, "I can't believe you were going to let him go!" Her tone was accusatory.

"I can't believe you ruined my big sacrifice."

She frowned. "What were you thinking?"

He could only shrug. "I wasn't thinking. When it came to it, I just couldn't arrest your brother. I think he knew I wouldn't be able to. In the end, he didn't play just you. He played me, too."

"He couldn't possibly have known that," she protested.

He gazed down at her and cupped her face in his

hands. "Maybe he knew both of us better than we knew ourselves."

Quinn draped an arm around her shoulder and guided her toward the airport exit. "Let's get out of here before things get messy."

"But Corbin," she sputtered. "The diamonds."

Something in Quinn's chest seemed to tighten at her indignation. "J.D. can handle it." Even as he said the words, more security guards were rushing through the terminal toward the gate. "Unless you want to spend the next twelve hours here while this all gets sorted out. Or would you rather go back to the house where you can tell me all about which of my qualities you love best?"

"Hey." She playfully bumped his shoulder with hers as he guided her toward the door. "What about all of my qualities that you love?"

He stopped just short of the door and turned her to face him. "Fearlessness." He pressed his lips to hers and kissed her soundly. "And generosity." He kissed her again. "And bravery." And again. "And your willingness to be pressured into a hasty marriage."

She pulled back before he could kiss her yet another time. "A hasty marriage?"

"I've waited almost fifteen years for our wedding night. I'm not waiting another minute longer than I have to."

She looked back toward the gate where her brother was being detained. "Don't you want to know what happens?"

"I already know what happens. I get the girl."

Epilogue

If anyone had asked her the week before, she would have sworn it was impossible to be so sublimely happy. Especially given that her brother was currently being returned to the States in the custody of half a dozen of Quinn's best men. Upon landing he'd be handed over to the stone-faced FBI Agent Ryan, who would handle things from there.

That, she was trying not to think about. Which was easier than it should have been since she and Quinn had been making love pretty much nonstop since they'd returned to the house alone. She'd slept some. They'd eaten a light lunch from the food scavenged from the pantry and deep freeze. Then they'd made love again.

There were a thousand things she wanted to ask him

about—after all, they had more than a decade of catching up to do. But for now, she was content to luxuriate in Quinn's company. She lay on the bed on her belly, arms folded around a pillow, waiting for him to return from a trip to the kitchen for more sustenance. She'd almost drifted off when she heard his footsteps entering the room. As she felt him sit on the bed, she rolled over, pulling the sheet to her chest as she propped herself up on her elbows.

He held a fisted hand out a foot or so above her belly and slowly opened his fingers, so what he held in his palm trickled out. It took her a moment to realize that what had landed on her belly was a stream of diamonds. The stones sparkled in the mid-afternoon light slanting through the window.

"Quinn!" she squawked in protest. "What on earth?"

He laughed at her response. "I believe I once promised to shower you with diamonds."

She plucked the stones from the sheet, worried she might miss one. "Well, I didn't think you were serious." She cupped the stones in her hand and extended it to him.

He folded her hand closed over the stones and met her gaze, his expression suddenly serious. "I need you to know I will always keep my promises to you. Every one of them."

She read the truth of his words in his eyes. He was with her to stay. She'd never be alone again. She got up on her knees and wrapped her arms around him. "I'll keep you to that."

Later, as she once again lay in Quinn's arms, though

the last thing she wanted to talk about was her brother—again—she still had to ask, "About what Corbin said back there…"

"About you not being alone?"

"Yes. Do you really think he planned on us getting back together?"

It didn't matter. Not really. She had Quinn and that was what was important. But somehow this business with Corbin might be a little easier to bear if he'd never intended for her to be all alone.

Quinn ran a hand over her hair, a motion filled with tenderness and love. She felt him nod. "I'd like to think he did."

"Me, too."

* * * * *

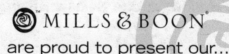

millsandboon.co.uk Community

Join Us!

The Community is the perfect place to meet and chat to kindred spirits who love books and reading as much as you do, but it's also the place to:

- ■ Get the inside scoop from authors about their latest books
- ■ Learn how to write a romance book with advice from our editors
- ■ Help us to continue publishing the best in women's fiction
- ■ Share your thoughts on the books we publish
- ■ Befriend other users

Forums: Interact with each other as well as authors, editors and a whole host of other users worldwide.

Blogs: Every registered community member has their own blog to tell the world what they're up to and what's on their mind.

Book Challenge: We're aiming to read 5,000 books and have joined forces with The Reading Agency in our inaugural Book Challenge.

Profile Page: Showcase yourself and keep a record of your recent community activity.

Social Networking: We've added buttons at the end of every post to share via digg, Facebook, Google, Yahoo, technorati and de.licio.us.

www.millsandboon.co.uk

2 FREE BOOKS
AND A SURPRISE GIFT

We would like to take this opportunity to thank you for reading this Mills & Boon® book by offering you the chance to take TWO more specially selected books from the Modern™ series absolutely FREE! We're also making this offer to introduce you to the benefits of the Mills & Boon® Book Club™—

- **FREE home delivery**
- **FREE gifts and competitions**
- **FREE monthly Newsletter**
- **Exclusive Mills & Boon Book Club offers**
- **Books available before they're in the shops**

Accepting these FREE books and gift places you under no obligation to buy, you may cancel at any time, even after receiving your free books. Simply complete your details below and return the entire page to the address below. You don't even need a stamp!

YES Please send me 2 free Modern books and a surprise gift. I understand that unless you hear from me, I will receive 4 superb new books every month for just £3.19 each, postage and packing free. I am under no obligation to purchase any books and may cancel my subscription at any time. The free books and gift will be mine to keep in any case.

Ms/Mrs/Miss/Mr_____ Initials _____

Surname _____

Address _____

_____

_____ Postcode _____

Send this whole page to: Mills & Boon Book Club, Free Book Offer, FREEPOST NAT 10298, Richmond, TW9 1BR